The Exchange Student's Secret

THE HEATHER REED MYSTERY SERIES

#1 *The Cryptic Clue*

#2 *The Model Mystery*

#3 *The Eerie Echo*

#4 *The Toxic Secret*

#5 *The Major League Mystery*

#6 *The Exchange Student's Secret*

The Exchange Student's Secret

REBECCA PRICE JANNEY

WORD PUBLISHING
Dallas • London • Vancouver • Melbourne

THE EXCHANGE STUDENT'S SECRET

The people and nation of Belgravia are fictional and in no way intended to represent actual people and events. They are products of the author's imagination, created and placed on a backdrop of Eastern European history.

Managing Editor: Laura Minchew
Project Editor: Beverly Phillips

Library of Congress Cataloging-in-Publication Data

Janney, Rebecca Price, 1957–
The exchange student's secret / Rebecca Price Janney.
p. cm. — (The Heather Reed mystery series ; #6)
"Word kids."
Summary: When sixteen-year-old Heather Reed and her family host an exchange student from Austria, Heather uncovers some startling facts about the girl's past that have significant implications for both teenagers and possibly an Eastern European nation.
ISBN 0-8499-3536-9 (trade paper)
[1. Mystery and detective stories. 2. Students, Foreign—Fiction.] I. Title. II. Series : Janney, Rebecca Price, 1957– Heather Reed mystery series ; #6.
PZ7.J2433Ex 1994
[Fic]—dc20 93-45623
CIP
AC

Printed in the United States

4 5 6 7 8 9 LBM 9 8 7 6 5 4 3 2 1

For my families: the Prices, Perios, Janneys, and Kurtzs

Contents

1

A Rude Welcome

"We're thirty-five minutes late!" Heather Reed moaned. "Of all days to get caught in a traffic jam. I hope Katarina's not upset by this."

Heather and her parents, Pat and Elaine Reed, hurried to find the gate where Katarina Schiller's plane was scheduled to arrive. The sixteen-year-old Austrian exchange student was coming to spend the fall school term with the Reeds.

"What a relief!" Heather exclaimed, looking up at the monitor that showed the schedules of arriving planes. "Her flight has been delayed. It isn't due for another twenty minutes."

"Wonderful!" Mr. Reed approved. "Let's relax and get something to drink. I'm all wound up after that traffic jam." He moved his head from side to side to work out the kinks.

The Reeds went to a snack shop and purchased four bottles of iced tea—one of them for Katarina in case she got thirsty on the way home—and three hot pretzels.

Philadelphia was famous for its soft pretzels, and these looked like good, fresh ones.

As they ate, Heather had an uneasy feeling that someone was watching them. She discreetly glanced at the other diners. A broad-shouldered man two tables away looked like he was reading a newspaper, but when Heather caught his eye, he seemed startled and quickly turned his back. She didn't get a good look at his face.

"Heather, what on earth are you staring at?" her mother scolded.

"It wasn't me, Mom," she said innocently. Then she lowered her voice. "That guy over there's been gawking at us."

"Honestly, Heather! Everything is a mystery to you! You're like a bloodhound on the scent of trouble." Mrs. Reed shook her head in dismay. Although she was proud of her daughter, Elaine Reed worried about Heather's safety.

"I don't think there's anything to be concerned about, Honey," Mr. Reed assured his wife. "We're with her. What could possibly happen?"

"You never know!" Heather's mother said ominously.

The sixteen-year-old stifled a giggle.

"Anyway, I can't blame him for staring," Mr. Reed continued. "After all, we have a lovely daughter."

Heather smiled at him in appreciation, then continued to glance discreetly at the man, who appeared to be in his twenties. *What interest could he possibly have in us?* Heather thought, twisting a piece of her long, honey-brown hair around her right forefinger.

"We'd better get to Katarina's gate," Mr. Reed prompted, interrupting Heather's thoughts.

They threw the trash from their snacks into garbage cans and walked toward the nearby waiting area. Heather looked over her shoulder once to see if the strange man was still there, but he was gone.

A huge 747 was just taxiing to an accordion-like tunnel outside the terminal.

"There's her plane now!" Heather pointed out.

"What timing," her dad grinned.

She took Katarina's photograph from her purse and looked at it for the umpteenth time that afternoon. The exchange student had thick, black hair that hung past her shoulders, and blue eyes that sparkled against a creamy complexion.

Mrs. Reed looked over her daughter's shoulder and smiled. "Pretty, isn't she?"

Heather nodded. "I think she looks real friendly, too."

One by one the passengers paraded into the waiting area, receiving hugs and kisses from friends and relatives. "I believe that's her now," Mrs. Reed announced, breaking into a big grin.

When the two teenagers caught each other's eyes, Heather waved, and Katarina waved back.

The tall, striking Austrian approached them a bit shyly. She carried a heavy-looking carry-on bag. "You must be the Reeds."

"Yes. Welcome to Philadelphia." Heather's mother hugged the girl. Then Mr. Reed awkwardly repeated the gesture, and Heather took her turn.

"You must be very tired," Mrs. Reed commented.

"Only a little. I had a good flight," said Katarina. She spoke with a charming accent.

"Let's get your bags," Mrs. Reed suggested. "Honey, how about if you get the van, and we'll find her things?"

"Sounds good to me," her husband agreed. "I'll meet you at the exit. Katarina, let me take your carry-on piece with me now." The exchange student gladly handed it over.

While Mr. Reed went for the minivan, the women made their way to the baggage pick-up area to get Katarina's luggage. They rented a small cart in order to more easily wheel the suitcases to the exit. Standing at the carousel with other travelers as they grabbed luggage from the conveyer, Katarina suddenly became agitated.

"Is something the matter?" Heather asked.

"Y-yes. That woman just took my suitcase!"

The two teenagers scrambled after the retreating figure who, fortunately, labored considerably with the heavy bag. A dumbfounded Mrs. Reed simply gaped as the girls hurried off.

"Ma'am!" Heather yelled, bearing down on the tall woman. When she only increased her pace, Heather caught the woman by the sleeve to slow her down.

"Pardon me, ma'am. I believe you took the wrong suitcase," she said directly. "This belongs to my friend."

Katarina looked down at the green bag and nodded. "Yes, that is mine."

"But it cannot be," said the middle-aged lady in accented English. "This is my suitcase," she defended.

The woman looked ready for a fight, so Heather tried a more diplomatic approach.

"Could it be that your suitcase looks like my friend's, and you took it by mistake?"

"Yes, that must be what happened." The lady stepped aside, and without another word, she rushed away.

"That's strange," Heather mused as she and Katarina headed back toward the carousel with the suitcase.

"What is strange?" asked Katarina.

"She didn't go back for her own bag. Katarina," she concluded, "I think she was trying to steal your suitcase!"

The Austrian's blue eyes widened in disbelief. "For what reason?"

"I have no idea," her American friend admitted.

"What happened?" Mrs. Reed hurried to their sides just then. The teenagers brought her up to date. "That's terrible!" she exclaimed. "Is that your only piece of luggage, Katarina?"

She shook her long, dark hair. "I also have a trunk to pick up."

They went back to the carousel where the crowd was thinning. Most people had obtained their suitcases and hurried away. Only a few pieces remained on the conveyer, but not Katarina's trunk.

"I wonder what could have happened to it?" she asked.

"Who knows?" Mrs. Reed threw her hands up. "Let's go report this to the airline people and see if it got left behind on the plane."

As they walked over to a special desk, the trio heard a woman scream, "Fire!" She was only a few feet away, and Heather ran in her direction. So did several other bystanders and a policewoman.

"What happened?" asked the officer.

"That man stole my purse!" she cried out, pointing to a retreating figure. "I heard that yelling 'fire' was the thing to do."

"That's right," the policewoman said.

As the officer went in search of the thief, Heather asked the victim if she had gotten a good look at her attacker.

"I'm afraid not," she sniffled. "Just that he was in his fifties maybe, tall and on the thin side. He had grayish-brown hair."

"Heather Reed, whatever are you doing?" her mother said, approaching them with Katarina by her side. "We've got to get that trunk and meet your father."

Her mother clearly meant business, and Heather quickly followed. But there was no trunk to be had.

"It doesn't seem to have arrived," a man at the counter for lost luggage said. "Let me have your name and number, and I'll call as soon as I get something on this. I'm very sorry, but this sort of thing happens from time to time."

"That is all right," Katarina said politely. "I am sure you will find it."

As they rolled her suitcase toward the exit, Heather said, "I hope you don't need anything in that trunk right away."

She shook her head. "I made certain to pack all necessities in my carry-on bag."

"I'm so glad you're here," Heather bubbled, putting the mysterious events behind her for the moment. She liked Katarina already. "I can't wait to introduce you to my friends and show you around school."

"Me, too."

They found Mr. Reed waiting impatiently at the exit. "Where've you been?" he asked his wife.

Quickly, she explained what had happened with Katarina's bag and the trunk. As Mr. Reed placed the suitcase in the back of the van, Heather returned the luggage caddie. She glanced around to see whether anyone was following her, but no one was as far as she could tell. Things finally seemed calm for the first time since the exchange student's hectic arrival.

After everyone was in the van, and they were driving away from the airport, Heather told her dad about the snatched purse.

"Well, Katarina, your trip has certainly begun in an exciting way!" he exclaimed.

Mrs. Reed said, "I forget, Katarina, have you been to America before?"

"No. This is my first time. My parents came here once, though." She suddenly realized the Reed family was incomplete. "Brian did not come?"

"He had a lab assignment due at school, but he'll be home for dinner," Heather said. "His roommate, Joe Rutli, will be with him, too. Joe practically lives with us during the school year. His father works in Belgium, so Joe stays with us whenever he's not living in the school dorm."

"How interesting! Which of Belgium's three languages does he speak?"

"He's taking German in school now. In fact, so am I."

"Sprechen sie Deutsch?" Katarina asked playfully. It meant, "Do you speak German?"

"Ich spreche kaum Deutsch," Heather smiled. That meant, "I don't speak much German."

"Heather's been working hard on the language to prepare for your stay," Mrs. Reed smiled. "She's been pouring over a German traveler's language guide for weeks now."

"I am so pleased," Katarina said. "I will help you with German if you will help me with my English."

"It's a deal," Heather grinned. "I have a feeling, though, that you'll be doing most of the helping. By the way," she said, changing the subject, "our next-door neighbors, Dr. and Mrs. Samra, are coming for dinner as well. They're like grandparents to Brian and me."

"Yes, you have mentioned them in your letters," Katarina said. "I loved hearing about your adventures with Dr. Samra. It must have been scary when he was missing and again when you were chased on his student tour of Israel.* I am excited to meet all your friends," Katarina continued. "By the way, you may call me 'Kat' if you like. I hear Americans like nicknames."

"We do," Heather said.

"What is yours?" she asked.

"According to my brother it's 'Trouble,'" Heather teased.

"What?" The dark-haired teen looked puzzled.

---

* Read about these mysterious adventures in *The Cryptic Clue* and *The Eerie Echo*.

Mrs. Reed said, "Once you spend a little time with my daughter, you'll understand."

Heather suddenly noticed that her father was glancing nervously into the rearview mirror. She turned around to find out what was bothering him. A male motorist in a navy-blue Lincoln was tailing the minivan. With him was a female passenger.

"I wish this guy would stop following so closely," Mr. Reed muttered.

Before anyone could reply, the Lincoln abruptly bumped into the back of the minivan!

"What in the world!" Mrs. Reed exclaimed.

The lanes had narrowed from four to two, and Heather's father wasn't in a position to let the luxury car pass. To his left, a concrete guardrail stretched along the expressway, while an enormous tractor trailer kept pace with the minivan to the right. In front of them, traffic was getting heavier and slower. It was not possible for the driver of the Lincoln to go around them.

Mr. Reed's jaw was set in a grim line as he considered his options. Suddenly the Lincoln shoved them from behind. Mr. Reed had to make a terrible choice—plow into the car ahead of him, ram the concrete barrier to the left, or drive straight into the tractor trailer's path!

2

Strange Beginnings

"Hang on!" Mr. Reed shouted.

His wife clutched the seat in fear, and Katarina was too stunned to say anything.

Mr. Reed skillfully kept the vehicle on a straight and narrow path, in spite of getting bumped two more times. Heather glared at the Lincoln's driver while trying to get a good look at his face. The man wore an old-fashioned brown felt hat and mirrored sunglasses. Because of the driver's head covering, she could only see the sides of his hair, but it appeared gray. Sun glare prevented her from seeing his passenger's face. The man's steel-like expression seemed bent on intimidation, and his thin lips stretched into a mocking grin as Heather watched him.

He's ramming us on purpose! she realized with a start. She attempted to get his license plate number, but the car didn't have a front tag. *It's a Pennsylvania-registered vehicle*, she concluded. *We only use rear plates*.

When the driver of the tractor trailer became aware of the Reeds' predicament, he slowed down, hoping to create enough space for the minivan to squeeze into.

Mr. Reed glanced to his right and saw the truck driver wave him into the narrow gap. Then Heather's father quickly darted into the right lane. She held her breath as the minivan fishtailed from the sudden acceleration and hit a steel guardrail on the road's shoulder. Then it came to an abrupt halt. The Lincoln disappeared into traffic.

Mr. Reed turned off the engine. "Is everyone all right?" His voice sounded strained. "Honey?"

"I'm a little shaken," his wife answered. "Thank God you avoided an accident, Pat. You did a wonderful job."

"Thank you. Girls?" He and his wife turned around to face them.

"I'm okay," Heather announced. "Kat looks pretty jolted, though. Are you hurt?"

"My neck is hurting a little."

Mrs. Reed, a pediatrician, climbed into the back seat and inspected Katarina's head and neck. "I think you have a slight whiplash." She took two pain-relief tablets from her purse and gave them to the Austrian, along with the bottle of tea they had bought for her earlier. "You can wash them down with this."

"*Danke*. I mean, thank you, Mrs. Reed." Kat smiled sheepishly.

Heather and her father got out of the van to inspect the damage while Mrs. Reed called the police on her car phone. Before they could take a look, though, a tan station wagon pulled up. A husky man in his twenties emerged from it. *He was the same man Heather had seen staring at them in the airport snack shop!* "Are you all right?" he asked, avoiding Heather's searching gaze.

"Yes, I think we are," Mr. Reed answered.

"I am glad. I saw what happened." The puzzling stranger shook his head disapprovingly.

"Thank you for your concern."

"My name is George Jones." He held out his hand, and Heather's dad shook it.

He has an accent, Heather noticed. Before she could ask Jones about it, however, her father spoke.

"Nice to meet you, Mr. Jones. I'm Pat Reed, and this is my daughter, Heather."

"It is good to meet you as well," he said, nodding politely at the teenager. When her eyes narrowed, he looked away. "Has your vehicle been damaged?"

"Let's look."

Together the trio inspected the minivan as cars and trucks whizzed frantically past them on the expressway. The front grill was slightly buckled, and the headlight on the right was badly smashed. In the back both tail lights were out, and the rubber part of the bumper was skinned.

"That isn't bad at all compared to what might have happened," Mr. Reed commented grimly. "That man was in such a hurry!"

Heather, however, didn't think that had been the case at all. She had seen the smirk on the driver's face. *But why did he do it?* she wondered. *And why did mysterious George Jones just happen to show up at the same time? Could they both have been following us?*

"It may help you to know that I saw the license plate and another identifying marker of the car that hit you," Jones offered.

"That's terrific!" Mr. Reed exclaimed. He pulled out his wallet and wrote the number down on the back of a business card. "And what about that other thing, that, uh, marker?"

"It was a decal that said, 'Liberty Bell Rentals.'"

Heather listened carefully as her father jotted down the information.

"Wonderful. Thanks so much." Patrick Reed held onto the card but stuck the pen back in his pocket.

"You are welcome," Jones said. "I am a mechanic and thought I might assist you."

"Where do you work?" Heather asked impulsively.

"In Kirby."

"Kirby! That's where we're from," her father smiled brightly.

Mr. Jones didn't appear to see anything at all out of the ordinary about the situation. "Yes. I work for Al Martino."

"Well, imagine that! He's our mechanic. I haven't seen you before," Heather's dad continued.

"I just recently started there," Jones answered. "It is, as you say, a small world." He looked meaningfully at Heather, and she stared back at him. Jones didn't flinch. He simply nodded and smiled a little.

"Pardon me, Mr. Jones," she said, "but I hear an accent. Where are you from?"

"Eastern Europe," he smiled.

"Then your real name isn't Jones," she remarked stiffly.

Her father wondered what she was up to now and regarded her quizzically.

"No, but my own is too difficult for most Americans to pronounce."

He smiled in a charming way, but Heather hardly noticed. She was too busy wondering why he didn't reveal his or his country's true identity.

"We have a friend in the van from Austria," Mr. Reed mentioned.

"Is that right?" Jones asked. Somehow he didn't look surprised.

Jones stuck around long enough to give a statement to the police when they came. Then he drove off in his station wagon. While Mr. Reed and the officer filled out an accident report, Heather stood there only half-listening. *I'm going to ask Al Martino about this guy,* she decided. *There's something about him that disturbs me.*

After completing the report, Mr. Reed started the minivan and again set out for home. When they finally arrived, everyone helped Katarina get settled in the guest bedroom upstairs.

"This is lovely," she said happily. Just then they all heard a loud thumping noise. Kat looked startled. "What is that?"

Heather laughed. "That's coming from my room. It's my rabbit, Murgatroid. She gets upset when she hears me and I don't pay attention to her."

"Oh, I want to see her!" Kat exclaimed.

"I'll leave you girls to yourselves," Mr. Reed said. "I need to report the accident to our insurance company."

That afternoon Heather helped Katarina unpack her suitcases. Before taking a nap, the Austrian called her mother to let her know she had arrived safely. When Kat awakened from her nap, it was five o'clock. She followed the sound of voices to the kitchen, where everyone had gathered while Mrs. Reed was preparing dinner.

"I hope you had a good rest," Heather said upon seeing Katarina. "How is your neck?"

"It is much better, thank you." She looked at the various people a bit shyly.

"I'm glad. Katarina, I'd like you to meet Dr. and Mrs. Samra; my brother, Brian; and his friend, Joe Rutli."

Joe looked like a goner when he laid eyes on the exchange student. Heather and Brian glanced at each other sideways and tried not to snicker at their friend's moonstruck expression.

"Now, would everyone please clear out, so I can finish dinner!" Mrs. Reed protested.

When they all sat down to eat a half hour later, everyone questioned Katarina about her life in Austria. Joe was especially attentive, and she seemed to like him, too.

"I have been to Belgium several times," she told him. "We traveled much in the summer for exhibitions."

"What kind of exhibitions?" Joe asked, leaning his chin on his palm.

"We have a horse farm in Krems, my hometown. My father taught students to compete internationally."

"He must be good," Joe commented.

Katarina answered quietly, "He was. My father died seven months ago."

Joe was too tongue-tied to say anything.

"He wasn't very old, was he?" Mrs. Reed asked.

The Austrian shook her head. "No. He was only forty-nine, but he had cancer."

"Didn't you mention in one of your letters that he was in the Olympics?" Heather inquired.

"Yes. He won a bronze metal in 1964," she said modestly. Her blue eyes were filled with pride, though.

"Do you have brothers or sisters?" Dr. Samra wanted to know.

"I am an only child," Kat replied.

"Like Evan Templeton," Brian teased his sister. Heather had recently started going to a lot of school and youth group activities with Evan. She rolled her eyes at her brother.

"What does your mother do, dear?" Mrs. Samra asked.

"She is an English teacher in what you call high school."

"So that's why you speak English so well!" Joe said.

"Thank you." Kat blushed from the compliment and Joe's obvious admiration.

Brian leaned over and whispered in Heather's ear, "He's got it bad!"

As she giggled in response, the phone rang. Heather jumped up to answer it. A minute later she returned to the table looking upset.

"What's the matter?" her mother asked.

"It was the airline calling about Kat's trunk. They want her to come right over to the airport. It seems they found it, but not before someone broke into it!"

3

Bizarre Theft

Poor Katarina! She felt weary from the long flight, and her neck was still sore from the accident. Now, someone had broken into her trunk! It really was too much. All the color had drained from Kat's face.

"Are you all right, Katarina?" Mrs. Samra touched the girl lightly on the arm.

Kat managed a faint smile and nodded. "I think so."

"Dad and I could probably see about the trunk without you," Heather suggested. "You've had an eventful day as it is." Mr. and Mrs. Reed agreed with the suggestion.

"That is kind of you, Heather. But I want to go and see what happened for myself. I cannot imagine why someone would break into my trunk. I did not have anything of great value in it."

"I suggest you finish dinner first, Katarina," Mrs. Reed instructed. "Then you may feel stronger."

The blue-eyed Austrian looked grateful. When the meal ended, she assured the Reeds that she felt well enough to go to the airport.

"Brian and Joe will help me clear the table," Mrs. Reed said when Kat began tidying up. Joe looked disappointed.

"I'll tag along, if you don't mind," Dr. Samra declared, pushing his chair back.

"Not at all, George," said Mr. Reed.

Since the minivan had had a rough day, too, Heather's father suggested they use his bronze-colored sedan. An hour later they were at the airport, where a middle-aged clerk led them to the trunk.

"It was on the same plane as Miss Schiller, but for some reason the trunk didn't make it to the carousel with the rest of her things," he explained. "When I checked it out, I noticed the lock had been jimmied open."

"Did you look inside?" Mr. Reed asked.

"No. Miss Schiller can tell us if anything is missing."

As Kat crouched beside her trunk to look inside, Heather said, "So someone probably forced it open on this side of the Atlantic."

The clerk nodded. "It wouldn't have gotten past the Austrian authorities with a picked lock."

Heather already had three suspects in mind—George Jones, the woman who took Kat's suitcase, and the hit-and-run driver. *It could even be that the passenger in that guy's car was the same lady who tried to make off with Kat's luggage!* Heather thought. *Somehow this must all be connected. Stuff like this doesn't just happen. I wonder what they're after?* It even occurred to her that the *what* might actually be a *whom,* as in Katarina.

"By the way, I asked security to check for fingerprints." The man shook his head. "There were so many from its being shipped, though, that they couldn't learn anything about the thief from what was there."

"Plus, the culprit may have used gloves," Heather pointed out.

A few minutes later Kat stood and frowned. "It is very strange. I can tell someone went through my jewelry because it has been shifted from where I packed it."

"That could have happened naturally in transit," Dr. Samra commented thoughtfully.

Kat shook her head. "The pieces have been moved to different containers."

"Is anything missing?" asked Heather.

"Only one thing is gone—my Bible."

"Your Bible!" Dr. Samra exclaimed.

"Why would someone want my Bible?" Kat mused.

"Whoever took it sure needed it," Mr. Reed remarked dryly, shaking his head in disbelief.

"You're sure nothing else was lifted?" The clerk seemed baffled, too.

"Lifted?" The word confused her.

"You know—stolen."

"Yes, I am sure," Kat stated. "Everything else is here."

The man summoned two workers to put the trunk in Mr. Reed's car. At first they thought it might not fit, but they managed to squeeze it in the sedan's trunk.

"I am so glad I always wear this ring," Kat said when they were back on the road.

Heather looked at the heavy, gold signet ring. Dr. Samra asked to see it. Kat took it off, something she said she rarely did.

"The ring belonged to my father," she told them as the history professor inspected it. "It has a fascinating story. He was born during World War II and grew up in a Swiss orphanage run by nuns. He never knew his parents or anything about them. The mother superior gave my father this ring when he left the orphanage at age eighteen. She explained that it was the only thing left to my father by his parents."

"That's some story," Mr. Reed commented as he stopped for a red light.

Kat smiled. "My father used to say the nun believed it might benefit him greatly someday."

"What did she mean?" Heather asked. She loved intriguing tales.

Her friend shrugged. "We never knew. My father used to tease my mother and me by saying it would bring us a great fortune." She paused. "To me it is worth more than any sum of money just because it belonged to him."

Dr. Samra handed the ring back, and Kat quickly put it on her finger. "That cross on the inside is the kind Orthodox Churches use. Was your father Orthodox?"

"No. He was Roman Catholic, as I am," Kat replied.

"Perhaps his family was Orthodox, though," the professor submitted. "Do you know anything about where they came from?"

"Nothing, I am afraid."

"As for the 'X' on top of the ring, it could be a family initial," Dr. Samra continued. "At any rate, it seems your ancestors were socially important people. The piece is exquisitely crafted."

"Maybe the trunk thief wanted that ring," Heather suggested. "Maybe your father wasn't kidding about its leading to a treasure."

"No one ever bothered about it before this time," Kat protested. "Besides, who else would know about the ring? My father never told anyone about it except me and my mother. He did not even wear it for fear of losing it."

"The thief didn't take any other jewelry, though," Heather stressed. "You had some pretty things in there, too. Since it was meddled with but no jewelry was taken, he—or she—might have been looking for something specific, like the ring." She paused momentarily. "Maybe that woman who took your suitcase was also searching for the ring," she guessed aloud.

"That seems far-fetched," her dad commented.

"But, Dad, she never returned to the carousel for her own luggage," Heather stressed. Mr. Reed nodded pensively.

Then Heather thought of something else. "Kat, was there a family tree in your Bible?"

"Yes, but it only contained information about my mother's relatives." She was obviously distracted. "Why would someone want my ring?" she returned to that subject. "No one ever troubled my father about it."

Heather pursed her lips. "I don't know, but I'd sure like to find out. Often family records are kept in Bibles, and that may be why the thief took it. I think your family may have a valuable secret!"

The next morning the Reeds, Kat, and Joe had a full breakfast, then they attended Sunday school and church together. Mr. and Mrs. Reed said they didn't expect the exchange student to go since they were not Roman Catholic.

"But I would like to see where you worship," Katarina insisted. So she went.

Heather took Kat to her Sunday school class and introduced the Austrian to Jenn McLaughlin, her best friend. Kat also met Jenn's new boyfriend, Pete Gubrio, and Heather's friend Evan Templeton. Later the five of them sat together in church. Afterward as the teenagers talked among themselves outside the sanctuary, an elderly woman approached them.

"I am Mrs. Borgoway," she said. "I am a Russian refugee and feel lonely for a European accent," she smiled. "It was good to know there was another one of us here today when the pastor introduced us as visitors."

"It is nice to meet you," Kat said politely.

Heather couldn't help but wonder what was going on. *It's not every day a Russian immigrant shows up at our church*, she thought suspiciously.

"Will you please an old woman by coming to tea this Tuesday after school?" Mrs. Borgoway asked. "You may bring your friends."

The girls agreed to stop by around four o'clock; the guys weren't interested and explained they had other things to do that day. As the woman gave them directions to her apartment, Heather thought, *I'm looking forward to learning more about this Mrs. Borgoway.*

Later that afternoon Heather took Kat on a walk through the Reeds' neighborhood. The temperature hovered pleasantly around sixty, and the leaves were just beginning to turn colors.

"This is a beautiful area," Kat said.

"I'm glad you like it," Heather responded. "It's a nice, safe neighborhood."

"Will you tell me more about some mysteries you have solved?" Her blue eyes shone eagerly. "I have been so excited to know all about them."

Heather had just opened her mouth when she suddenly caught sight of someone darting between two houses midway down the block.

"Did you see that, Kat?" But before the other girl could answer, the most vicious dog in the neighborhood came tearing across a lawn and headed straight for them!

4

Up a Tree

"Oh, Heather!" Katarina screamed.

"Follow me!" Heather shouted. "That's Haman, the meanest dog in the neighborhood."

An elderly neighbor kept the dog for protection, but he always locked Haman securely inside a fence. Unfortunately, the gate was now swinging open, giving the snarling beast free run of the neighborhood.

Heather grabbed Kat's arm and propelled her toward an oak tree. Then she shoved Kat upward, and the Austrian pulled herself onto the first limb. Quickly she moved up another branch to make room for Heather. She scurried to safety just in the nick of time. Haman had lunged upward, tearing into the bottom of Heather's jeans with his sharp fangs.

"Heather, be careful!" Kat yelled, panic-stricken.

Quickly, Heather tore off a smaller, leafy branch and waved it in front of the dog's eyes, hoping to distract him. It worked! The brute let go of her jeans in confusion, and Heather scrambled further up into the tree.

But the two teenagers still weren't totally out of danger. The tree wasn't a mature one, and its branches couldn't support the girls for long. *I'll bet we only have a few minutes at most before these limbs snap,* Heather thought grimly. In the meantime, Haman had begun barking and snarling even more furiously.

"What do we do now?" Kat's voice trembled as Haman's noisy barks filled the air.

"Hang on!" Heather advised, quietly praying for their rescue.

Just then Mr. Sewell, Haman's owner, appeared in his doorway. He took one look at the situation and hurried across the yard as fast as his legs would go, shouting and waving his arms. "Haman!" he shouted. "Heel, Haman! Heel!"

The dog, still yelping, turned first toward his master, then proudly in the girls' direction. He seemed to be saying, "I caught them for you!"

"It's all right, Haman. They're friends. Heel!" cried Mr. Sewell, seizing the dog's collar. The elderly man led a reluctant Haman back to his fenced-in yard.

Heather and Kat descended from their perches and dropped to the ground. Mr. Sewell hurried back to them, full of apologies.

"Are you girls all right?"

"Yes," Heather replied. "Thanks for rescuing us."

"I am so sorry about Haman. I can't imagine how that gate got opened. I checked on it just fifteen minutes ago, and it was secure."

"Do you keep it locked?" asked Heather.

The elderly man shook his head. "No, but I will from now on. I hope you'll give Haman another chance," he said quietly. "He is a good watchdog."

"I won't report you, if that's what you mean, Mr. Sewell. It wasn't your fault."

After introducing the man to Kat, Heather told Mr. Sewell about the mysterious person she had seen just before being chased up the tree. "He probably let Haman loose."

"Whatever for?" Mr. Sewell cried out.

Heather shook her head. "That's what I'd like to know."

After the elderly neighbor apologized several more times, the girls said they needed to be going.

"I'd like to ask some neighbors if they saw that person release Haman," Heather told Kat as they walked away.

"You make it sound as if someone did this on purpose," she objected. "Why?"

"I'm not sure," Heather admitted. "Kat, I hate to say it, but some strange things have happened since you got here yesterday."

"I know. What should we do?" She looked bewildered.

"We'll have to keep our heads up." When Kat looked perplexed, Heather smiled. "It means, 'be careful'. Something unusual is going on, and I want to find out what it is."

When they got back to the house, Kat told the Reeds about Haman. Heather's parents were understandably upset. Joe said he'd like to teach the wise guy who let Haman loose a lesson. Although no one said it, everyone was thinking what Heather had expressed to Kat earlier—that curious events had occurred since her arrival.

After a light supper of vegetable soup and chicken salad sandwiches, Brian announced that he and Joe were going back to school. "How about giving us a lift, Heather? You'll probably want the car this week to show Kat around." They shared a red sedan.

"That'll be great," Heather said. "Thanks. By the way, Kat, on Sunday nights I go to a youth meeting at my church."

"Yes, I heard some talk of it this morning," she said.

"You're welcome to come. But if you'd rather not, I won't mind."

Kat smiled. "I would love to go. I like your friends very much."

"Then we'll drop the guys off at school and go to the meeting from there."

When they arrived at Brian and Joe's red brick dorm, the guys hefted their backpacks and two large bags full of clean laundry from the trunk.

Joe hesitated. "You still have a half hour before youth group starts," he commented. "Would you like to take a walk around campus?" he asked Kat.

"I would like that!" she exclaimed. It seemed she also liked Joe.

While Heather parked the car, the guys dropped their things off. Then they met the girls outside on the porch. The tour lasted longer than Heather expected. Joe seemed determined to show Kat the entire campus. When Heather caught Brian's eye and pointed to her watch, he understood.

"Joe, I think they need to get going," he announced. "Come over when you have more time, and we'll show you the whole place, Kat."

At the youth meeting, the group of about thirty played several volleyball games. Kat only watched, since her neck still hurt a little from the accident. When the matches ended, everyone went to the youth lounge for refreshments and a brief devotional talk. Then the gathering broke up for the evening.

"I'm still hungry," Pete complained as they walked out into the crisp, autumn air.

"Me, too," Evan chimed in. "I know! Let's all go for a pizza."

"I think that's a terrific idea," Jenn agreed. "I'm always hungry. Is that okay with you, Kat?"

"Yes." Her face glowed. "It will be my first American pizza. You may think it is silly, but I have looked forward to this."

"Let's see," Evan teased. "Where should we go?"

"How about Gubrio's?" Pete said as if on cue. His Uncle Tony ran a pizza shop on the other side of Kirby.

They decided to leave Heather's car in the church parking lot and take Evan's beat-up Bronco. It wasn't a lot bigger than the sedan, but it was more fun. All five teenagers crowded inside. On the way they talked and sang, laughing and enjoying one another enormously.

When he saw his nephew and the others, Tony Gubrio's pleasant, round face lit up. "Pete! Hey, it's good to see you."

"Hi, Uncle Tony. I hope you have lots of pizza ready—we're hungry!"

"For you, always!" he joked. "Who are your friends?"

"You know Jenn," Pete's face flushed slightly.

"I sure do," his uncle teased.

"And this is Heather Reed and Evan Templeton."

"Hi, kids. How are youse?"

"Great!" they laughed.

"Who's the new girl?" Tony asked slyly.

"This is Katarina Schiller. She's an exchange student from Austria, and she's staying with the Reeds."

"Nice to meet ya!" he grinned. "I hope you like it here. Now, what'll youse have?"

They had already made up their minds on the way there. They ordered a large pizza with everything but anchovies.

"How about a pitcher of root beer to go with it?" Tony suggested. "On the house!"

"Sure!" they all said, except for Kat.

"I did not know American teenagers could drink beer," she whispered into Heather's ear.

"It isn't alcoholic, Kat," she explained. "It's a soft drink."

"Have a seat, and I'll be right with youse," Tony instructed.

When they got settled around a table close to the counter, Kat asked, "What does *youse* mean?"

The others reared back their heads and laughed. When he stopped chuckling Pete explained, "Some people in this area use it to mean *you* in the plural."

"If you hang around the Reeds long enough, you'll hear them say y'all," Evan cut in. "That's how some Southerners say the plural of *you.*"

"In Pittsburgh they say *youns,*" Jenn mentioned.

"But *you* is plural, is it not?" Kat asked.

"It is," Heather replied. "It just seems that some people think it needs to be enhanced."

"I have much to learn," Kat giggled.

"You're doing fine," Evan assured her.

A half hour later as the pizza rapidly disappeared, the conversation became more high-spirited. Pete loved telling jokes. They were even funnier after explaining them to Kat. Unfortunately, something happened that abruptly cut off their laughter. Two people in black, their faces obscured by full ski masks, charged into the pizza parlor. One of them grabbed Tony Gubrio by the collar and pointed a gun at him.

"Listen up everybody!" the intruder announced in a husky, muffled voice. "Put your jewelry in the hat, and no one will get hurt. If not, . . ." he growled and pointed the weapon straight at Tony's heart!

5

Pizza Shop Holdup

Heather inhaled deeply, trying to keep her wits about her. Several thoughts shot through her mind like speeding cars. *I'm sure this is happening because Kat's here. These guys might just be after her ring. Why else would they want our jewelry? It isn't at all valuable. I'll try to stall them.* Heather watched them carefully, looking for anything that she could use to identify them to the police.

"You heard me!" the gunman snarled, waving the weapon at Tony. "Hand it over!"

Pete's uncle looked more than scared as sweat began dripping from his forehead. His face seemed a bit greenish, as if he might get physically sick.

I think he has a heart problem, Heather remembered with alarm. *God, please strengthen him. Don't let the strain be too much for him.*

The youths reluctantly began taking off their jewelry as the accomplice hastened to their table. Heather had thought up a plan and gave each of her friends a look that said, *Move slowly*. She demonstrated by taking off her earrings as if in slow motion.

As she unbuckled her watch band, Heather studied the thieves more closely. The one at their table was tall, but wore baggy clothes. Heather couldn't tell if it were a man or a woman. Plus the ski hats hid everything but their eyes. The gunman had piercing hazel eyes, and the other one's eyes were brown. When Heather dumped her watch into the hat, she thought the brown felt fedora looked familiar. She couldn't place it, however.

This is the second time I couldn't tell if a suspect was male or female, she noted.

"Hand it over," the thief holding the hat demanded in a suppressed voice.

They're trying to conceal everything about themselves, Heather continued her inner reflections. *Even their voices. It sounds as though they might have accents, but I can't make them out clearly.*

Katarina stared sadly and reluctantly at the unusual ring she wore. Noticing this, Heather "accidentally" bumped Kat. When she got her attention, Heather shook her head as discreetly as she could. Kat caught on and slowly undid the clasp on her inexpensive watch, avoiding her ring until the last possible moment.

"Hurry up!" the accomplice shouted impatiently.

That is a woman's voice, Heather thought.

But this discovery produced no excitement. She feared there wasn't enough time to save Kat's precious ring. Just as Katarina began to remove the priceless object, however, Police Officer Mike Armgard wandered through the door. The sight of him startled the gunman so badly that he dropped the weapon, sending it clamoring loudly to the floor. Motioning to his cohort, they fled out a side door near the counter, also leaving the hat behind. It took the officer only a second to realize he'd interrupted a holdup. Instantly, he took off after the criminals.

Tony Gubrio slumped against the counter, and Pete rushed to his side. Heather hurried over to the phone and called 911. "There's been a holdup at Gubrio's Pizza Parlor on the far end of Main Street going west," she said. "The owner also has a weak heart, and I think he's having trouble with it."

With Evan's help, Pete got his Uncle Tony to a chair. "Is he okay?" Jenn came over and asked with deep concern.

"I think so," Heather said. "Jenn, please try to keep people from crowding him."

But there was no need. Officer Amy Weaver, Armgard's partner, hurried inside and took over. An ambulance arrived soon thereafter, and more police. Two other officers rushed to assist Armgard while paramedics put Tony Gubrio on a stretcher.

"I'll be all right," he told Pete. "Tell Aunt Joan not to worry, okay?"

"Sure." He turned to one of the medical technicians. "Where are you taking him?"

"Pottstown," she answered. "Want to go along?"

"Uncle Tony?" he asked.

"That would be fine. Would your friends close up for me?"

"We'd be glad to," Evan announced.

"Show him the keys and what to do with the money," Tony instructed weakly. "Make sure to shut off the oven and put the food away."

"Hurry up," the paramedic said. "We'll be leaving soon."

It didn't take long for Pete to show Evan and Heather how to close the shop. He had worked for his uncle before and knew the procedure well.

"That was a close call!" Jenn's voice trembled after they left with sirens blaring into the night. She seemed on the verge of tears.

"It was so frightening," Kat agreed, looking shaken.

"Are you girls all right?" Officer Weaver asked them.

"Yes," Kat and Jenn stammered. Heather knew Officers Weaver and Armgard from earlier cases she'd helped solve.

"Heather Reed, I might have known you'd be here! Tell me exactly what took place."

The teenager quickly explained what had happened, pointing out the gun and hat still lying on the floor. The officer picked them up carefully so as not to destroy any fingerprints.

By now all the customers were talking excitedly about their narrow escape, and Amy Weaver began questioning them.

Before long, her disappointed partner returned from his chase, announcing that the thieves had gotten away. Then he turned to Heather. "Fancy meetin' you here!" In spite of his gruffness, Armgard was glad to see her.

"Hi," she grinned impishly.

A half hour later, as the police finished taking statements, Heather took Armgard and Weaver aside. "I'd like to know what you find out about the gun and the hat."

"I don't doubt it," Armgard sputtered.

"Call the station in a few days," Amy Weaver said with a knowing smile.

The following day Katarina went to her new school for the first time. Heather, Jenn, Evan, and Pete did their best to acquaint the Austrian with Kirby High. They wanted everything to go well, especially since Kat's stay had been such a disaster so far. They had already received some good news that morning. Tony Gubrio was feeling better and would be coming home from the hospital in a few days. Then they all discovered happily that at least one of Kat's four new friends would be in each of her classes.

In spite of the good news, though, Heather still looked forward to the final bell. She had investigative work to do.

When Heather and Kat got home, Mrs. Reed and Mrs. Samra were in the kitchen. They wanted to know all about the exchange student's first day of classes.

"I'm glad you had such a nice time," Mrs. Samra said after hearing how well school had gone. "You needed one! Mrs. Reed told me about the dog and the holdup." The grandmotherly neighbor shook her head and clucked her tongue. "Sometimes I wonder what this world is coming to! Well, I must be going."

"Thank you so much for shuttling me around today, Miriam," said Mrs. Reed as she walked her friend to the door. "I don't know how I would have managed otherwise."

"How long will the minivan be in the garage?" Heather asked after them.

"Probably a week," her mother answered. "That Mr. Jones you met when we had the accident was there when we took it in. He was very nice."

Heather wasn't so sure. *I'm going to ask Al Martino about him,* she determined. But first she wanted to check out something else.

After Mrs. Samra left and Kat went upstairs to put on more comfortable clothes, Heather called Kirby Police Chief Andrew Cullen from her room. He was a long-time friend of her family. Heather often asked for his advice about the mysterious incidents that she seemed forever to be running into. And he always patiently listened to what she had to say.

"Well, Heather Reed!" he exclaimed. "Armgard and Weaver told me about last night's holdup. Might this call have anything to do with that?"

"Sort of," she answered. She told him all that had taken place since Katarina's arrival on Saturday. "I just wish I knew who that hit-and-run driver was," she concluded.

"How about I give the rental place a buzz?" he offered.

"I'd sure appreciate that. The Lincoln had a Liberty Bell Rental Car sticker on it."

"I'll check into it later this afternoon when I get some free time," Chief Cullen promised.

The police chief returned the call just after dinner that night. "I found out that the Lincoln was rented to a guy named Carl Reitz. They gave me his phone number, but when I tried it, I found it was no good. Guess what else?"

"What?" Heather's voice trembled with excitement.

"He gave a phony Philadelphia address, too."

"Wow!" she exclaimed. "Did he pay the bill?"

"Sort of. He used a stolen credit card."

Heather thought quickly. "Did you trace the owner?"

"Sure did. The name, Carl Reitz, was right. The card was stolen from his wife's purse at Philly International on Saturday."

"You're kidding!" Heather exclaimed. Then she told Chief Cullen about the purse-snatching she had witnessed. "So that woman was probably Mrs. Reitz?" she asked.

"I would think so," he agreed.

Heather had one of her sudden inspirations. "Chief Cullen, I just remembered something! You know that accomplice in the pizza parlor holdup?"

"Yeah?"

"He was using a brown felt hat just like the one I saw that guy posing as Carl Reitz wearing in the Lincoln." She paused as he whistled.

"I'll keep my eye out for this guy. Why do you think this stuff is happening, Heather?"

She lowered her voice. "I'm sure it has something to do with our exchange student. I have this feeling someone wants a certain ring she wears." Heather told the chief what she knew about it, then added, "What do you think?"

"I think you might be on to something."

6

Cookies and Bombs

The following day Heather sat next to Katarina in their Global Governments class, their next-to-last one of the afternoon. Their interesting teacher, Mr. Michaelson, was getting ready to show a special video he had put together of recent evening news reports.

"There's a big conflict brewing in a small Eastern European country called Belgravia. It's a beautiful country with rich natural resources and wonderful skiing." He sighed. "Now it's in danger of becoming a war zone. Actually that whole area is in trouble. The Belgravians have been trying to establish a new government since the old communist one fell apart. In a few days there will be free elections, and the outcome will determine Belgravia's future."

The instructor flipped off the lights and showed the class his tape. Afterward they discussed it.

"Katarina, you're from Europe," Mr. Michaelson said after several minutes of dialogue. "Have you ever made it to the eastern part?"

"Yes. I actually have been to Belgravia."

He became excited. "Tell us what you saw."

"It was a few years ago, and I do not remember a great deal about the trip," she admitted. "I was about twelve years old, and we went for a horse show."

"A horse show?"

"Yes. My father had a horse farm, and he taught young people to compete," Kat explained. "We went to a European-wide contest in Belgravia. They have a reputation for their excellent horses and trainers."

"Were you in the contest?" he questioned.

"Yes," she said modestly.

"So, what was your impression of Belgravia?"

"Well, I remember the country seemed gray. The people were nice to us, but they did not seem happy," she reflected.

"Did you take pictures?" Mr. Michaelson asked.

"Yes, but I do not have them with me. They are home in Austria."

"Thank you, Katarina."

"Mr. Michaelson," Heather raised her hand.

"Yes, Heather?"

"What kind of government do the Belgravians want now?"

"Many of them want a monarchy again. They had a queen until the end of World War II. But even now some people want another communist state where the government rules with an iron fist."

"Why would they want to do that?" asked another student.

"For one thing, it represents stability for many of those who are hungry and jobless. Those people feel that at least they had work and small apartments to live in under the communists. They got used to having the government do everything for them." The loud ringing of the bell interrupted him. "That's it for today. Don't forget, we'll be having a test soon."

After school, Jenn joined Heather and Katarina for a brief meeting of the Environmental Awareness Club. They were grateful for its brevity because of their promise to meet Mrs. Borgoway at four o'clock. When the meeting was over, the girls got into Heather's car and drove to the Russian woman's apartment complex. She looked overjoyed to see them.

"An old woman gets lonely, especially when she is by herself and new to a place." She took their jackets and hung them in a hall closet. Then she invited the teenagers to be seated in her modestly furnished living room.

Heather glanced around. The apartment had a combination living-dining room, small kitchen, and she guessed, probably one bedroom and bath. The country-style decor didn't fit her image of what would suit the tastes of an elderly, Russian woman.

Mrs. Borgoway brought a tray of delicious-looking cookies and tiny cakes from her walk-in kitchen.

"They look beautiful!" Jenn exclaimed. "Did you make these?"

"Yes," Mrs. Borgoway smiled. "Please eat as much as you like." Then she threw her hands up in dismay. "I have forgotten the sugar bowl!"

"I'll get it," Heather quickly offered. She jumped up and went to the kitchen before the woman could protest. Heather found the sugar bowl on a bare counter next to a bakery box with extra cookies and cakes. *I wonder why she lied about baking them,* the teenager thought.

"Have you found it, dear?" Mrs. Borgoway called from the living room. She sounded a bit nervous.

"Yes," Heather said, bringing in the cut-glass container, trying to look casual. After accepting a cup of tea from the elderly woman, Heather asked, "When did you come to Kirby?" She caught a glimpse of Jenn happily munching away. Heather also noticed that Kat didn't take anything.

"Only recently," said Mrs. Borgoway.

"What brought you here?"

"I watched an old way of life die in Russia. I was fearful for my future there," she told them dramatically.

"But you are all alone here," Katarina remarked. "Have you no family in Russia?"

The woman shook her head sadly. "I have no one. My husband is dead, and we did not have children. My brothers and sisters are gone as well."

"I think that's so sad," Jenn said, reaching for another cookie. "I hope you'll like it here."

"I think I will," Mrs. Borgoway said. Then she turned to the Austrian. "Please eat something, Katarina."

The girl managed a weak smile. "No, thank you. My stomach hurts me today. But I will have some more tea."

"I am sure that will help settle your stomach," Mrs. Borgoway said, pouring a cup.

Heather found herself intrigued by the woman's energy level. *She seems so lively to be a tired, old woman who's alone in the world*, she observed. *Jenn and Kat seem to like her a lot, but for some reason, I don't think Mrs. Borgoway is genuine.*

"What made you come to Kirby?" Heather inquired, selecting a spiced cookie with sugar sprinkled on top.

Mrs. Borgoway smiled shyly. "I am certain you will think it silly of me. You see, I have always liked the pictures of Philadelphia I've seen in books. Yet I do not like the noise of cities. I wrote to the Philadelphia Chamber of Commerce and asked for a list of its suburbs. I thought Kirby sounded like a wonderful place in which to spend my last years."

"Was it difficult to move all your things?" Heather asked, thinking it truly was an odd explanation. She was determined to learn as much as she could about the woman, especially after all the weird stuff that had happened since Kat's arrival.

"I had very little to bring besides my clothes and a few items of personal value. The furniture came with the apartment," she explained wearily. Before Heather could ask more questions about Russia, Mrs. Borgoway addressed Katarina. "And how do you like it here, my dear?"

"I have met many good people," Kat said politely.

She didn't mention the minivan episode, her trunk being broken into, Haman's attack, or the pizza parlor incident. The Austrian teenager did not wish to offend her American friends. Jenn, however, told Mrs. Borgoway about the holdup at the pizza parlor.

"I am sure that was traumatic for you girls," the woman clapped her hands in dismay. "I have heard there is much crime in America."

Kat fingered her ring. "I am just relieved that the thieves did not steal this."

"Oh?" Mrs. Borgoway's eyebrows lifted slightly.

"My father died seven months ago. He left me this ring."

"May I see it?" the woman asked.

Oh, no! Heather inwardly groaned. *I wish she hadn't done that.*

The exchange student held her hand closer to Mrs. Borgoway's eyes so she could see the gold ring. As the woman examined it with great eagerness, Kat told her the story behind it.

"It must mean a great deal to you, then," the older woman commented, appearing to be easygoing about the whole thing. Heather had a hunch it was all an act, that Mrs. Borgoway was really quite interested in the object.

She nodded. "I consider it priceless."

"Yes, it is," her hostess agreed.

At 5:15 Jenn said she needed to get home, so the girls thanked Mrs. Borgoway and rose to leave.

"I am so glad you came," she said. "I do hope you can do it again."

As the Russian woman reached into the closet for their jackets, Heather noticed something strange—a man's trench coat. *It sure looks like a guy's,* she thought. *I wonder why it's in there.*

Mr. and Mrs. Reed were making dinner when Heather and Kat got home. The teenagers told them about their interesting visit with the Russian immigrant.

"I hope you don't mind, Mom and Dad, but I had cookies at Mrs. Borgoway's, and I don't feel like eating anything else just now. May I be excused?" Heather asked.

"Of course," Mrs. Reed answered. "How about you, Katarina?"

"I am not hungry. I would like to do my homework."

"That means a romantic dinner for two," Mr. Reed said, hugging his wife playfully.

The girls retired to their rooms to do school assignments. At eight o'clock Kat knocked on Heather's door and said she wasn't feeling well.

"What's wrong?"

"My stomach is upset, and I am cold," Kat explained.

"Sounds like you're coming down with something," Heather guessed. "I'll tell Mom."

Mrs. Reed came upstairs and examined Kat. She said, "I think you may be getting that flu that's going around. It wouldn't surprise me. Your resistance is probably low from all the traveling and adjustments you've made in the last four days."

"I am so much trouble to you!" Kat complained.

"Nonsense," said Mrs. Reed. "Now go to bed. I'll check on you in a little while. If you need me before then, give a holler."

"Give a holler?" Kat scrunched her eyebrows. "What is a *holler?*"

Heather laughed. "It means, 'call me.'"

On Wednesday morning, Kat wasn't well enough for school, so Heather promised to get notes for her. But she couldn't keep the pledge. At 11:45 a secretary summoned her from algebra class.

"Your father's waiting for you in the office," she said as they walked down the hall.

"My father! What's going on?" Heather was instantly on red alert.

The woman shook her head. "I don't know."

When Heather saw her worried dad in the office, a lump formed in her throat. "What's wrong now?" she asked.

"I thought it best to take you home just in case," Mr. Reed said mysteriously.

"In case what?" Heather was beside herself with curiosity.

He sighed heavily. "In case someone may be after you, too."

She couldn't stand the suspense. "What happened?"

"A bomb exploded at the house."

7 Ordered Home

"Was anyone hurt?" Heather asked fearfully.

"Not as far as I know. Let's go, Heather. I'm anxious to get home."

He thanked the secretary for her help, and they left the school building. Once they got in the car and began the brief trip to the house, Heather started asking more questions. She wanted to know everything that had happened.

"Mom called my office forty-five minutes ago with the news," he began. "She said the incident occurred fifteen minutes before that." Mr. Reed, managing editor of *The Philadelphia Journal*, worked in the city.

Heather calculated quickly. "So it happened an hour ago."

He nodded. "Your mother was quite upset, as you can imagine. She didn't say much, just that a bomb went off, and I should come home at once."

"Where did it explode?" Heather had a vivid image in her mind of the house blowing up.

"In the front yard."

She breathed a sigh of relief. "Thank God." Heather paused, then said, "I wonder who did it, and why?"

"Hopefully we're about to find out."

Minutes later they pulled onto their street, but Mr. Reed couldn't get into the driveway. Police cruisers filled it, and the yard had been roped off. They quickly got out of the car, slamming the doors behind them.

"Wow, Dad! Look at that hole in the yard!" Heather cried out.

He gave a low whistle as they advanced toward it. The bomb had ripped into the beautiful lawn, creating a massive, ugly crater. Fragments of dirt had showered the downstairs windows and white siding of the house, making it look like an abstract painting.

"Hey, Pat, what happened?" a concerned neighbor asked Mr. Reed. A few others gathered around him and Heather.

"I'll let you know later," he answered. He grabbed his daughter's hand and pulled her gently toward the house.

"Pat! Heather!" a familiar voice yelled.

"There's Mom!"

Heather and her dad hurried toward Mrs. Reed, crossing the police barricade easily because Officer Armgard was protecting the house. He nodded somberly to them.

As Heather followed her parents inside the house, her dad asked, "Was anyone hurt?"

"No one." Mrs. Reed's answer relieved him. The three Reeds went to the living room, where Chief Cullen and Officer Weaver were with the housekeeper and Katarina.

"So, except for the lawn, the house is okay?" Heather asked.

"That's right."

"Did the bomb squad come?" she persisted.

"Yes, they were here, but there wasn't much to be done. The bomb had already gone off," Mrs. Reed explained a bit breathlessly. "They investigated and took its remains to the police lab."

Chief Cullen rose as they entered the room. Both Kat and the housekeeper, Ella Freemont, appeared distressed. After subdued greetings, everyone sat.

"I think we'd better take it from the beginning," the police chief announced. "Mrs. Freemont, suppose you tell us everything just as you remember it."

"Well, Katarina was resting upstairs. She was home today because she was sick with the flu. I had just gone up to see if she needed anything when there was a knock at the front door." She took a deep breath and continued. "When I got there, a brown National Delivery truck was pulling away. The driver motioned to a package he'd left on the porch. The delivery people have never left a package in that way before. It made me feel a bit suspicious.

"Tell me how the parcel looked," Chief Cullen requested.

"The box felt strange when I picked it up. It was light in some places, then heavy off to the side."

"To whom was it addressed?" Officer Weaver asked.

"'Miss Katarina Schiller.' I took it to her, and she opened it."

Chief Cullen interrupted her. "Then what happened, Katarina?"

The teenager trembled as she recounted the frightening story. "I lifted the lid and inside were broken cookies. Then there was a square object, like a clock, and it was ticking. Mrs. Freemont yelled, 'A bomb!'"

The housekeeper interrupted to give her version of what happened next. "I grabbed the box and ran to Heather's room. Then I opened the window and threw the whole thing onto the lawn. When it hit, the bomb exploded." She held her hand to her heart. "I got the window down just in time."

"Where were you, Elaine?" Chief Cullen asked Mrs. Reed.

"In my office downstairs. Fortunately my patients were all inside; no one was on the lawn when the bomb exploded."

"What happened after that?" Heather asked anxiously.

"I called 911," Mrs. Freemont said. "The police came right away."

"This is awful!" Mr. Reed exclaimed. "Who would try to do such a dreadful thing to Katarina?"

"That's what I'd like to know," Chief Cullen said darkly. "Describe that box again, Ella."

"Like Katarina said, there were crushed cookies inside," Mrs. Freemont repeated.

Before she could go on, however, Heather cut in. "Homemade or store-bought?"

The stout woman narrowed her eyes. "Why in the world would that be important?"

"Every detail is," Heather said respectfully. Her instincts told her this could be a critical clue.

"Well, I think they were bought cookies. What was left of them had that look."

"And the box?"

"It was white, wasn't it Katarina?"

She nodded. "Yes, it was. And it was wrapped in brown paper."

"I think it's absurd that someone would send cookies with a bomb," Mrs. Reed retorted.

"I take it there was no return address?" Andrew Cullen asked.

Both Katarina and Mrs. Freemont shook their heads.

"I think we ought to call National Delivery and check out the driver," the police chief decided. "May I use your phone?"

Mr. Reed took Cullen to his study just off the living room. The officer returned five minutes later with some important news.

"Wait 'til you hear this! That guy was driving a stolen truck. An hour or so before the explosion, the real driver went inside a King of Prussia business to deliver a package. When she returned, the truck was gone."

"But the man was wearing a company uniform," Mrs. Freemont protested.

"Did you see the driver clearly?" Cullen asked her.

"Not really," she admitted. "He seemed on the older side of fifty, though."

"What makes you say that?"

"Although he was wearing a company cap, I could see some gray hair under it."

"That should help. Weaver, you and Armgard see if you can track down that truck. I'll finish here."

Officer Weaver nodded, said good-bye, and left.

"I must get back to my patients," Mrs. Reed announced as she got to her feet. "Will you be needing me any longer?"

"No thanks, Elaine," Chief Cullen said. "Mrs. Freemont, you can go, too. I'll let you know if I need anything else from you."

"Well, I'll be glad to help in any way I can," Ella Freemont responded. She followed Mrs. Reed out of the living room.

After they left, Chief Cullen turned to the exchange student with a serious expression. "Katarina, do you have any idea why someone might want to hurt you?"

That's exactly what I'm wondering, Heather said to herself.

"I do not know why at all," Kat hung her head. "I am very upset by this. I have caused so much trouble for the Reeds."

"I can imagine how upsetting this is to you, Katarina," Cullen remarked. "Someone must have known you stayed home from school today."

"That person was likely watching the house," Heather stated quickly.

Chief Cullen nodded. "Precisely. But that still doesn't tell us why. It sounds like you have some enemies, Katarina."

"I do not," her blue eyes flashed. "I cannot think why someone would want to hurt me."

"I heard about the hit-and-run, the trunk, the dog, and the pizza shop holdup," the police chief said, looking sharply at Kat. "Those things do not just happen."

Katarina's lower lip quivered. "Do you think I am a dishonest person?"

"I've never met you before. I'm just looking at all the angles," he explained.

"I still think someone may be after Kat's ring," Heather concluded.

"What makes you say that?" Cullen asked, leaning back in his chair.

"Mostly because of how the trunk thieves seemed to be searching for a particular piece of jewelry. They rummaged through it all but didn't take any. Why else would they do that?" she explained.

"That sounds like a long shot," her father spoke up for the first time. He had been deep in thought.

"Maybe not," Chief Cullen remarked. "This is, after all, a strange case."

Heather also mentioned Mrs. Borgoway's and George Jones's sudden appearances in Kirby.

"It sure sounds unusual to me," he scratched his head.

"Kat, did anything peculiar happen to you before you left Austria?" Heather questioned.

"No," she started shaking her head slowly, then abruptly changed her mind. "I did not think two times about it until just now."

Heather smiled at Kat's funny way of saying, *I didn't think twice about it*. "What happened?"

"I was in a bookstore a week before I left Austria looking for a certain book to bring with me. I needed the ladder to reach it. It was attached from the floor to a runner high up on the wall," she explained. "When I climbed it, the ladder began to sway. Then it came loose, and I fell."

"Were you injured?" Heather asked.

"Just a little bruised."

"Of course, it might have been an accident. But in view of what's happened since you arrived in the States, I suspect you were being followed back home, too," Cullen said. "Has anything been unusual in your life recently?"

Kat said quietly, "My father died seven months ago. That is all."

"Sorry to hear that," he said. "Well, if you come up with anything else, call me." The officer plucked his hat from his lap and got up to leave.

"Chief Cullen, did you learn anything more about the hat and gun the pizza parlor thieves left behind?" Heather asked quickly.

"Oh, yeah. The guy who rented the Lincoln bought the gun in Philadelphia with the same stolen credit card."

Heather became excited. "Then he's our prime suspect?"

"Sounds like a good lead," her dad responded.

"Yeah, but finding him could prove very difficult," Chief Cullen cautioned. "He's a slippery one. By the way, about that hat. It didn't have a label inside or any other way we could trace it. But I will say I haven't seen any like that around here for ages. My dad used to wear one when I was a kid. And that was a long time ago," he laughed.

"Say, Kat, do men wear hats like that in Austria?" Heather asked.

"I sometimes see older men with them, but a younger one would never wear such a hat."

Before leaving, the police chief strongly suggested that Katarina call her mother. "I think she would want to know what's going on."

When Kat made the transatlantic connection several minutes later, her mother was so upset she demanded that her daughter return to Austria at once. Even Kat began thinking she should leave.

"I am causing so much trouble for you," she told Mr. Reed as he stood nearby.

However, after talking to Mr. Reed at length, Kat's mom agreed to let her daughter stay another week to see if the troubles would be resolved by then.

After Chief Cullen left, Heather went to her room, wrestling with a troubling thought: *What if Kat isn't as innocent as she acts?*

8

Stepped-up Investigation

It didn't take long for Heather to lay her fears to rest. *Kat seems genuinely baffled and disturbed about what's been happening. She just doesn't strike me as the criminal type. I honestly doubt she's done anything wrong.* Then a new idea occurred to her. *Maybe Kat was an eye witness to something illegal! Anyone could get an enemy that way.* Heather sighed just the same. *That doesn't address the theft of her Bible, though, and any possible connection that has to her ring.*

She decided on the direct approach. "Can we talk, Kat?" Heather asked moments later as she stood in her new friend's doorway.

"Yes. Please come in," she invited. Kat had been writing an essay at her desk and put it aside.

Heather sat in an oak rocker and shared what was on her mind. She wasn't sure where to begin and got off to a bad start. "I'm trying to figure out this mystery. It occurred to me that you might be hiding something," she said.

Kat's blue eyes widened in disbelief. "I have done nothing!" she objected. "If you do not believe me, . . ."

"No, no," Heather waved her hands. "I didn't mean you're dishonest, Kat. I'm simply wondering whether you witnessed a crime back home, and if someone has threatened you because of it."

"No, Heather, I did not." Katarina hung her head slightly. "I fear you really do think I have done something bad."

Heather said more tactfully, "I admit that the thought crossed my mind awhile ago, but I don't think you're that kind of person," she added quickly. "I do trust you."

"I am glad to hear that. I assure you, I am honest and have no reason to have enemies. I am so puzzled by these events." She began crying softly.

"Trust me, Kat. I'll get to the bottom of it." Heather leaned over and patted her friend's knee.

"You have just one week," she declared. "Can you possibly solve this mystery in such a short time?"

Heather pledged to do her best. For the next hour they went over the essay Kat was working on, then Heather excused herself. She went to her room and called Chief Cullen, hoping he had further news. He did.

"Armgard and Weaver found the delivery truck twenty miles north of town."

"That's wonderful!" she exclaimed.

"Yep."

"I suppose it was abandoned," Heather guessed.

"You suppose correctly, but our suspect left a great clue behind."

"What is it?" she asked impatiently.

"His uniform."

"I wonder where he got it in the first place," Heather mused.

"What do you make of that, junior detective?" he asked playfully.

"I wonder if costume shops rent those uniforms?" she guessed. "National Delivery is the best-known service in the country, so I think that's possible."

"Good thinking, Heather. I'll have someone check it out in the next few days." Heather knew Chief Cullen would take care of it, but Kat was running out of time.

"Is there anything else you can tell me?"

"Nope. Listen, Heather, whatever you do, be careful, huh? You have a way of getting into the thick of things."

She laughed. "I know, and I will."

On Thursday Katarina felt well enough to attend school, but by three o'clock she was feeling very tired and weak. So when Mrs. Reed asked Heather to drive her to Martino's Auto Body to pick up the minivan after school, Kat asked to be excused.

"I think that's wise," Mrs. Reed said. "You're still on the mend. We'll be back shortly."

Heather looked forward to questioning Al Martino about George Jones. In all the recent excitement, she had forgotten to call him about his new employee. To her disappointment, however, Al had gone to run an errand and had left Jones in charge.

"Is he coming back?" Heather asked.

"No. Mr. Martino said he would go straight home," Jones said. He turned to Mrs. Reed and smiled. "The repairs cost less than we estimated."

"Well, isn't that unusual!" she stated, looking at the bill.

While her mother began writing a check, Heather asked the mechanic, "How do you like your job?"

"It has been very helpful," he said.

"Helpful?" *That's a strange answer,* she thought.

"Yes. I have learned a lot about people in my work," he answered mysteriously.

"I'm curious. Which Eastern European country are you from?" Heather was hoping to catch him off guard.

"It is hard to say."

"Why?" she asked point blank.

"There has been much unrest in that region. I do not know to which country I will return someday," he responded.

"Do you mean like Belgravia?" Heather questioned, thinking of her recent Global Governments class.

"That is a country in turmoil."

Could he be one of the criminals chasing Katarina? she wondered. *He's acting weird enough*. She looked at him more closely. *Jones seems bigger than either of the pizza parlor thieves, though, and he's only in his twenties. Where and how does he fit into this mystery?*

Heather tried another approach. "I recently met an elderly woman at my church who comes from Russia. Her name is Mrs. Borgoway. Do you know her?"

George Jones got a peculiar look in his blue eyes. "I do not think so."

"I thought maybe she was a customer, too."

"Perhaps she is," he answered cryptically.

He held Heather's gaze for a moment. Just as she thought of another question for their cat-and-mouse discussion, Mrs. Reed tore the check from her book and handed it to him. "There you go! Now, if you'll give me my keys, we'll be on our way. Let's go, Heather. I have patients coming."

As she walked to the door, the young man called after Heather, "Let me know if you need anything."

On the way home she tried making sense of the conversation. *He must know something about what's going on. Jones wouldn't tell us his real name before, and this time he refused to reveal his country. I think that's odd. And why would he ask me to let him know if I needed anything? I'm going to ask Chief Cullen to keep an eye on him. Even if George wasn't involved in that holdup, he might still be working with the others.*

Then she thought of something else, something in Jones's favor. *Why did he come to our rescue on the Schuylkill, though, if he's out to get Katarina? I suppose he could have wanted to get that ring, but then the police came, and he couldn't.* But she wasn't sure at all.

When Heather got home, she called National Delivery and asked if any costume shops carried replicas of their uniforms.

"Yes, and it's a dreadful nuisance," the man on the phone retorted.

"Do you know which stores?" she asked.

"No, I don't," he grouped.

Heather thanked him and hung up. *I guess the thing to do is make a list of costume shops in the area, then call to find out if any of them sells those uniforms. From there I can ask if any were rented recently but not returned.*

But first Heather phoned Chief Cullen and asked if he knew anything about George Jones or Mrs. Borgoway.

"Are they suspects in the Kat case?" he questioned.

"Uh-huh. They're both recent immigrants, and I wonder whether they could be illegal ones. Is there any way I can find out?"

"Hmm. That might be difficult for you. But since it involves Katarina's case, I'll check them out."

They spoke for a few more minutes, then Heather hung up. Next she called Al Martino's home and was very glad when he answered the phone. Heather explained that she was interested in knowing more about George Jones.

"Why, Heather, you surprise me!" he exclaimed. "I'll admit he's good-looking, but he's a few years too old for you right now," he teased.

"Uh, that isn't the reason I'm asking," she said quickly. "What is his real last name?"

"Bolevic."

"Did he tell you why he uses Jones?"

"He says it's easier," Al said.

"That makes sense," Heather admitted. "How is his real name spelled?"

"B-o-l-e-v-i-c," he clarified.

"And the end is pronounced, *vich?*"

"Uh-huh."

"Do you know where he's from?" Heather pursued.

"Switzerland."

She couldn't have been more surprised. "Switzerland! With a name like Bolevic!"

"Maybe he moved from somewhere else. He doesn't talk much about it."

"Are his working papers in order?" Heather asked.

"They sure are. I always do a thorough check before hiring anyone."

"Thanks for your time, Al."

"Hey, is my employee part of a new mystery?" He seemed tickled by the idea.

"I'm not sure," Heather said.

"Well, let me know if I can do anything else for you," he offered.

"Thanks." Heather hung up and picked up her pet rabbit. "Murgatroid, this is getting pretty confusing."

Because she had a lot of homework due the next day, Heather put off calling costume shops until school was out for the weekend. Then she ended up postponing the task again when Katarina said she wanted to do something special after school Friday.

"I feel well again and would like to have some fun," she said.

"Maybe we could go to the movies," Jenn suggested. "Do you like them?"

"Yes, and I have heard about your huge theater complexes. I would like to see one." Kat seemed excited by the idea. Then her expression went sad. "It may be my last chance."

"Don't worry," Heather reassured her. "We'll get this mystery solved before your week runs out."

"I hope so," she returned.

"You can count on Heather," Jenn said proudly. "There's nobody like her for solving a tough mystery."

"What's up?" Pete Gubrio asked as he and Evan caught up with them at the flagpole.

"We're trying to decide which movie to see tonight," Heather said, glad that Jenn's praise had been cut off.

"Are guys allowed?" Evan teased.

"Only if we don't see some shoot-em-up or slasher film," Jenn frowned. "They give me nightmares."

They decided on an adventure-romance everyone was talking about. Evan offered to pick the girls up at Heather's at 7:15 to make the 7:40 showing. Pete said he couldn't go; he was helping out at the pizza shop until his uncle got back full time. That night at the Reeds' dinner table, Joe Rutli expressed an interest in going along.

"Hey, Brian, maybe we could go, too," he said hopefully.

Heather smiled to herself. *Anything to be near Kat! Of course, Jenn wouldn't mind having Brian round out the party. She'd had a crush on him for years.*

"I guess I could use the break," Brian admitted. "Although I hate to get behind. I've got some tough classes this semester."

"Ah, c'mon," Joe coaxed.

"If it's okay with the girls."

"We'd love to have you come," Heather smiled.

That evening they all enjoyed the movie. Since it was only 9:30 when it ended, they began looking for something else to do.

"I know! Let's get a pizza," Joe said as they stuffed themselves into Evan's Bronco. Everyone groaned in unison. "Oops! I forgot about the holdup!" He clapped a hand over his mouth. "We could get some burgers at the drive-through window and go somewhere special to eat them."

"I'm all for that," Brian said.

So were the rest. They went to a fast food restaurant, ordered their food, then headed toward Valley Forge Park to eat their meal near the memorial arch.

When Evan pulled into the park, however, the scene before them was anything but inspiring. He was heading up the two-lane road into the main section of the park when the car behind them pulled out to the left lane to pass.

"What in the world!" Brian grumbled. "This is a no-passing zone."

"There's a car coming straight at him!" Jenn shouted.

9

Unmasking the Criminals

"Steady, Evan," Heather said. "Just keep it steady."

Evan slowed the Bronco to a crawl to avoid getting mixed up with the other two cars. The oncoming sedan swerved wildly to its right to prevent a collision with the aggressive driver of a maroon Cavalier who had passed Evan's Bronco. But it was too late. The Cavalier grazed the sedan's front bumper, propelling it toward a steep embankment! The offending car sped from the scene of the accident.

Heather tried unsuccessfully to make out the brutal motorist's features, but he had whizzed by before she could get a good look. However, she noticed he had no passengers. *Oh, I hope those people in the sedan are all right!* she worried.

Evan pulled the Bronco to the side of the road. "Let's see if anyone's hurt," he said.

"Their car is tipping sharply over the hill," Jenn fretted.

"We'd better help them get out," Brian said, climbing out of the Bronco. He didn't add what he was thinking, *Before it's too late.*

"Let's go!" Joe exclaimed, and everyone followed.

Just then a tan station wagon pulled up behind the Bronco. Before following the others across the road, Heather paused to see what was up with the wagon. When the driver got out, Heather froze in her place. It was none other than George Jones!

"George! What are you doing here?" she gasped.

"I often seem to find you like this," he said. His rugged face wore a serious expression. "Is everyone all right in your vehicle?"

"Yes, we're fine," she said impatiently. "Where did you come from?" Her tone was confrontational. *This is one coincidence too many!* she thought.

"I was behind the car that darted out so foolishly into the no-passing zone. It was terrible of him to run off like that." Jones shook his head in disgust.

"So the driver was a man?" Heather asked. Jones nodded. "Did you get a good look at him?"

"He was an older man with graying hair," he said stiffly.

"What about the license plate?" she inquired.

"I saw and wrote down the number, as well as the make and model of his car. I will call the police."

With that he got back into the wagon and drove away.

Heather hoped he would keep his word. When she crossed the narrow road, she saw her friends trying desperately to free a family of four from the sedan before it pitched over the steep embankment. Evan, Brian, and Joe pushed against the back end of the car to keep it from rolling down while Jenn and Kat helped the family out safely.

Heather rushed to help. With all of them working together, they got the parents and their two children to safety. Then, while the mother comforted her children, the father, Heather, Kat, and Jenn joined the guys. With a mighty effort they managed to shove the car back onto level ground.

A few minutes later, as everyone regained their strength, Evan walked over to Heather. "Who were you talking to?"

"A guy named George Jones."

Katarina overheard them. "George Jones!" she exclaimed. "What was he doing out here?"

"That's just what I would like to know," Heather commented.

"Where did he go?" Evan asked.

"To get help."

As if on cue, sirens split the night air, announcing the police and rescue team's arrival. For the next half hour officers questioned the young people and the family about the hit-and-run accident. Because of the late hour when they were finished, Heather and her friends went straight home.

"Oh, yuk!" Jenn complained. She held up the large bag of cold burgers and stale fries.

The others started to laugh. "Umm, my favorite snack," Joe teased.

"Are the drinks still drinkable?" Brian asked. "I'm parched after that effort back there."

"They look watered down," Jenn announced, lifting the lid on one large cup.

"Hand it over, please," Brian requested. "Wet is wet at this point."

"That was some adventure!" Joe told Kat.

"I have had so many adventures since coming here," Kat said. Her voice sounded unsteady.

"At least this one had nothing to do with you," Joe soothed.

Heather wasn't so sure. *Why was George Jones there?* she wondered. *Was he following us? If so, why?* She felt especially suspicious about the hit-and-run nature of the mishap. *I have to admit, though, both times he was on the rescuing end of the incident. What does it all mean?* For now, there were no answers.

The next morning after breakfast, Jenn wandered across the street from her house to the Reeds'. Heather told her and Kat she wanted to find out what area costume shops carried replicas of National Delivery uniforms. "I'll ask those who do if a customer rented one recently and didn't return it."

Katarina volunteered her help. "If someone wants to hurt me, I will not take it in my seat."

Jenn burst out laughing, and the Austrian blushed. "I have done it again."

"I think you mean *sitting down,*" Heather giggled.

"I should not use American expressions. I make them sound so foolish," Kat said.

"Not at all!" Jenn blurted. "I love the way you talk. I think it's so cool."

"Me, too. And I'd love to have your assistance," Heather added. "You and Jenn can help me look through the phone books to get the names and numbers of costume shops near Kirby."

Just then Joe appeared in the doorway. "What's going on?" he asked. He and Brian had spent the night there.

When Heather explained, he volunteered to help. "Do I have time for breakfast?" He had already showered.

"Sure," Heather said.

"I will make you something," Kat offered. "I love to cook. Have you eaten, Jenn?"

"Yes, but I'm still hungry," she sighed. "Unfortunately I'm always hungry."

"While you guys eat, I'm going to make a phone call. Then we can get those names and numbers and start calling."

Heather went to her father's study and called the Kirby police. "Hello, this is Heather Reed. May I please talk to Chief Cullen?"

"I'm sorry, he's not in right now," said the dispatcher.

"How about Officer Weaver?" she tried.

"I'll connect you."

A minute later a voice said, "Hello, this is Amy Weaver. How may I help you?"

"Hi, Officer Weaver. This is Heather Reed." She told the policewoman about the "accident" at Valley Forge Park.

"That must have been awful," Weaver sympathized. "When I think of what you've been through lately, I really feel for you and your Austrian friend."

"It was pretty scary. I thought Chief Cullen should know about it because of everything else that's been going on."

"I'm sure he'll appreciate that, Heather. Thank you for calling."

Heather hung up the phone and rejoined her friends in the kitchen. Brian was there with them, eating omelets and joking around.

"Want something?" Jenn asked.

"No thanks."

"Why so glum, Heather?" Joe questioned.

"I'm thinking hard," she explained.

"Uh-oh," Brian groaned. "When that happens, watch out!"

His sister did what she usually did—ignored him. "When we get those costume shop numbers, we can call half the stores from here and the others from Jenn's, if you don't mind." She looked questioningly at her friend.

"Not at all. Kat, you can come with me, okay? I'd like you to meet my family anyway."

"I would like that," the Austrian smiled.

Joe looked a little disappointed, but he behaved like a good sport. "I'll give you a hand over here, Heather."

"Thanks, Joe. Brian, I don't suppose you will?" she asked her brother.

"Sorry, sis. I've got a big test Monday."

"All work and no play, Brian," Joe warned.

"I'm afraid I am a dull boy right now," he quipped.

After breakfast the foursome found the names of thirteen costume stores. Then they paired off to call the places, agreeing to meet back at the Reeds' kitchen when they were finished. Heather and Joe took turns calling their seven shops and had no success until the fifth call. The manager at the King of Prussia Mall store said they rented the delivery costumes, but they didn't have every size available—one of the outfits had not yet been returned!

"Bingo!" Joe yelled. "Should we tell the others?"

"Yes." Heather called Jenn's, but even after several tries, she couldn't get through. "They're still calling places. We'll have to wait."

When Jenn and Kat finally came back saying they'd had no success, Heather told them she had.

"Now what do we do, Heather?" Joe asked.

"Let's go to the mall. Maybe the manager can tell us something about the guy who rented the outfit. Maybe she can lead us to him!"

"Then the mystery will be solved, and Kat can stay!" Jenn exclaimed.

Heather wasn't so sure it would be that easy.

At the mall costume shop Heather asked for the manager. "I called earlier about a National Delivery outfit," she told the woman.

"What size do you need?"

"Actually I wonder if you could tell me about the one that hasn't been returned?"

The woman narrowed her eyes. "Why?"

"We'd like to know who rented it."

When the manager hesitated Jenn said, "Please. It's very important."

The woman looked through her invoices and found the one for the delivery costume. "Let's see. There isn't a name." She frowned. "It's two days overdue, and there's no name and no charge account number. I told that new part-timer to get that information."

"What about a deposit? Don't you require those?" Heather asked.

"Uh-huh. This guy put one down, but it must have been with cash. Stupid clerk." The woman was obviously upset with the person who had taken the order. "If the items aren't returned, the cost will come out of her paycheck."

Heather explained that the Kirby Police Department had retrieved such a uniform, and she might check with them.

"I don't get it," the manager regarded them curiously.

"It's a long story," Joe smiled.

"Did the person rent anything else?" Heather asked.

"Let's see," she looked. "Yes, a gray wig was also rented. Of course, that hasn't been returned either."

The teenagers left the store and wandered up to the food court, pleased with their discovery and ready for lunch.

"I'd like to use the rest room first," Heather said. "Do you want to come with me?" she asked Jenn and Kat.

They didn't. "We'll wait here for you," Jenn said.

Heather walked past several food counters, sniffing the mouth-watering aromas of pizza, hot dogs, steak sandwiches, and Mexican food. *I'm hungry for a cheese steak,* she decided.

In the rest room several minutes later, Heather reached for a paper towel to dry her hands. Suddenly someone seized her from behind. She opened her mouth to yell, but a hand clamped firmly over her entire face so that she couldn't see her attacker or cry for help. A muffled voice growled, "Mind your own business, Heather Reed!"

The assailant shoved a container under Heather's nose. Almost instantly, sickeningly sweet fumes overcame the teenager, and she blacked out.

10

Flea-Market Clue

The next thing Heather knew, someone was saying, "My dear, please wake up!" As she began a slow climb back to consciousness, the faces around her appeared blurry. Then she gradually realized she was sitting down, and several people were talking about her.

"She's coming to!" Jenn shouted. "Heather, can you hear me?"

She nodded dully.

"Stand back and give the poor girl breathing room!" a mall security guard commanded. Then he asked Joe, "Would you like me to call an ambulance?"

"No ambulance," Heather managed to say thickly. "I'm okay." She suddenly knew where she was—on a bench in the food court. As her mind cleared, she was surprised to see Mrs. Borgoway hovering over her.

"Oh, thank goodness you are all right!" the elderly woman cried out. "I was so afraid." She chewed nervously at her fingernails.

"But how . . ." Heather's voice trailed off.

"I went into the rest room and found you unconscious just inside the door," Mrs. Borgoway explained. "It gave me such a fright. I went for help, and the guard brought you out here where your friends were waiting."

Once Heather felt like herself again, she went with her friends to file a report with the mall security office. Mrs. Borgoway had left after being questioned briefly.

When they finished their report, Heather asked, "Did anyone see my attacker leave the rest room?"

"Not that we know of," a guard who had just come into the crowded room said. "We talked to the food court staff and some diners, but no one reported seeing anyone suspicious. Could you identify the person?"

"I didn't get so much as a glimpse." Heather felt glum.

After the questioning, they all decided to eat lunch someplace else and drove to a nearby diner. When they got home at 3:30, Joe and Kat told Mr. and Mrs. Reed about Heather's encounter at the mall. Although Heather kept assuring them that she felt fine, they were beside themselves.

"What next?" Mrs. Reed mumbled. "Heather, I want you to go upstairs and lie down for a bit. You may feel all right, but you had a nasty experience, and you need some rest."

On Sunday Kat decided to go to Mass at the Kirby Roman Catholic Church, instead of going with the Reeds to their church service.

"I would still like to go to your youth meetings, though," she told Heather, then sighed heavily. "That is, I will go if I am still in Kirby. Oh, Heather! Do you think you will find the answer to all this strangeness before I have to return home?" she asked hopefully.

"I think so," Heather smiled. "Let's have faith. Sooner or later these crooks are going to trip themselves up."

After the morning service at the Reeds' church, Mrs. Borgoway made a fuss over Heather. "Oh, I do hope you are all right, my dear. That was just terrible."

"I'm feeling fine."

"Is this the woman who found you?" Mrs. Reed asked.

"Yes." Heather introduced her parents, Brian, and Joe to Mrs. Borgoway, and they chatted for a few minutes. Then they said good-bye and walked out to the minivan in the parking lot. *I think it's strange that Mrs. Borgoway just happened to be at the mall at the same time we were and that she was the one who found me,* Heather considered. *I wonder if she had anything to do with attacking me in the first place? I just don't trust that woman. I wonder why she and George Jones are following us around?*

As her dad started the engine and pulled out of the parking lot, Heather continued thinking about the assault. *The person who grabbed me was pretty strong. Mrs. Borgoway's too old to have a grip like that. Plus, the voice was too muffled for me to identify—just like the accomplice in the pizza parlor holdup!*

When Brian complained loudly, he roused Heather from her daydream. "Ah, Dad, I'd really rather not. Besides, I have that test to study for."

"What's going on?" she asked.

"Dad wants to take Kat to a flea market," Brian explained.

Heather groaned. She and her brother didn't share Mr. Reed's passion for outdoor sales.

"It's a wonderful way to see grassroots America," Mr. Reed defended. "I bet she would love it. And it may be our last chance to take her someplace special like that," he added sadly.

"Oh, I do hope those dreadful people are found before something else happens," Mrs. Reed worried. "I can't blame Katarina's mother for wanting to bring her home."

"The thing is," Heather added, "I'm not so sure she'd be any safer there than she is here."

"What do you think this is about?" her dad asked.

"I still think it has something to do with Kat's ring. Maybe it's the key to a fortune after all."

"Then why would someone attack you, Heather?" her mother asked.

"I guess to get me out of the way."

Brian interrupted. "Uh, Mom, Dad, about that flea market. I really have to . . ."

"I know, 'study for that test,'" Mr. Reed said. "Joe, what about you?"

"I'll go if Kat does," he said brightly.

Heather stifled a laugh. *Joe would do anything to spend time with Katarina*, she thought playfully.

When the Reeds got home and Heather's dad told Kat about the flea market, she eagerly agreed to go.

"We have those in Austria, but they are not as big as what you have described," Kat said.

Although Heather wasn't eager to go, she decided to make the trip anyway in order to be with Kat. After changing their clothes and eating a quick bite of lunch, Mr. and Mrs. Reed, Heather, Kat, and Joe drove north on Route 29 to the giant Perkiomenville flea market. Kat was astonished by the variety of items people were selling, from discarded paperbacks to nostalgic lunch boxes that cost upwards of one hundred dollars.

"Some prices look so good, but others are too high," Kat observed, holding an old mirror in her hand. "This is just two dollars and very pretty."

She was delighted when Joe bought it for her.

"About the only things I look for are pretty tea cups and saucers for Jenn," Heather said. "She collects them."

"I like those, too," Kat agreed.

While Mr. Reed buried himself in a box of ancient magazines and his wife prowled around antique furniture, the teenagers went off on their own.

Joe and Kat stopped to admire some brilliantly colored potted mums, but Heather was attracted by a table with china. She strolled over and discovered several modestly priced tea cups she was sure Jenn would like.

"Need help?" a stocky woman asked her.

"How much are these?" Heather couldn't find any prices.

"Seven dollars apiece. Genuine antiques."

"Thank you." While the woman went to another potential customer, Heather picked up an unusual cup and saucer that had caught her eye. Each piece was a beautiful onyx color with heavy gold bands around the rim. When she turned them over to find out where the set had been made, Heather noticed writing from a different alphabet. Although she couldn't translate the odd letters, her heart raced. The pieces also bore the same fancy "X" that appeared on Katarina's ring!

11

The Mysterious Symbol

"Where did you get this?" Heather asked breathlessly.

She hoped the clerk might know something about the pieces, something that could help Heather solve the baffling mystery surrounding Kat.

The woman told her, "I picked them up at another flea market. Now where was that?" She put a finger to her lips and thought for a few seconds. "I know!" she snapped her fingers. "It was near Cincinnati, Ohio."

"Do you know anything else about the cup and saucer? Anything?" Heather pressed for information.

She regarded Heather curiously. "No. Why?"

"It's so unusual," she said innocently.

The clerk got a shrewd look on her face. "I'll sell it to you for ten dollars."

"Ten! But it was only seven a minute ago," Heather objected. *She thinks I'll pay more because of my interest,* she thought.

"That was a mistake. It's obviously more valuable than the others," the woman explained sweetly.

They bartered in a lively fashion for several minutes. In the end Heather bought the set for eight dollars. Then she hurried to another aisle where Kat and Joe were browsing through books.

"Look what I found!" she called out. "Does this look familiar, Kat?"

The Austrian became very excited when she saw the cup and saucer. "I have never seen anything besides my ring bearing that symbol. What do you think it means?"

"Kat, I believe your ring is more precious than you realize. I also have a feeling this mystery may soon be worked out," Heather stated.

"Oh, I do hope so!"

"Maybe you should put the ring in a safe-deposit box, Kat," Joe suggested.

"I think that's a great idea," Heather approved. So did her parents when they learned what had happened.

When the group returned from the flea market, they displayed their purchases to Brian.

"Show him the cup and saucer," Joe prodded Heather.

She handed them to her brother saying, "The words remind me of Russian. Can you tell what they mean?"

Her brother had taken a Russian-language class in school and done well in it. He picked up a magnifying glass from his dad's desk and closely examined the letters. Everyone else crowded around, eager to know the cup and saucer's background and what connection it might have to Kat's ring.

"This isn't Russian," he finally announced, "but it could be one of the languages derived from Russian." He paused then added, "I think it may say, 'Made in Belgravia.'"

Belgravia again! Heather thought.

"Sweetheart, do you have any connection to that country?" Mrs. Reed asked Kat.

"No, I do not," she shook her head decisively.

"You said your father was a war orphan, right?" Heather asked.

"That is right."

"And you don't know where he came from before he was taken to Switzerland by the nuns?"

"No."

"Maybe he came from Belgravia," Heather suggested.

"I think that's possible, given his childhood situation," Mr. Reed said. "You know, Katarina, that ring may represent a war-time inheritance that someone knows about and wants for him- or herself. That kind of thing has happened a lot in Eastern Europe in the last few years."

"Another relative might know about it, but you said your father didn't have any, right, Kat?" Heather asked.

"Yes. That always saddened him greatly."

Mrs. Reed put her hands on her hips. "Tomorrow that ring goes into a safe-deposit box. I will not let it jeopardize you any further, Katarina."

"I would like to do that," she agreed.

"I have an idea," Brian said. "Tomorrow night at school, a Swiss professor will be giving a public lecture. She teaches Russian History and will speak on Eastern Europe. She probably could tell us what those words say."

"Excellent idea!" his father approved. "I think we should all go."

After school on Monday, Mrs. Reed took Katarina and Heather to the bank where the mysterious ring went into a safe-deposit box. When they got home, Heather made another investigative phone call. She wanted to know if the airline knew anything more about the person who had broken into Kat's trunk.

"I wish we did, but nothing has turned up," the manager said. "We just don't have much to go on. I'll call if anything breaks, and of course, we'll pay to replace that Bible if we can't recover it."

Next, Heather called Officer Weaver and asked if she had found out anything about Friday's hit-and-run driver.

"Only that his car was rented and paid for with a stolen credit card," she said. "We haven't caught up with the guy yet, but we have a description. He is in his fifties, somewhat tall, and has graying brown hair."

Heather was excited. "I see a pattern emerging." Then she told the policewoman about the Carl Reitz episode.

After hanging up, Heather went to Kat's room. "Do you have a minute?"

"Yes," she smiled shyly. "I am afraid you caught me reading a book when I should be doing my homework."

"Well, I think you're so smart it won't hurt," Heather commented. "What's the book about?" She sat on the edge of Kat's bed.

"It is a fascinating story about Anastasia."

"Hmm. Is that about the woman who claimed to be the last Russian czar's daughter?"

Kat nodded. "Yes. She claimed to have escaped miraculously when communists murdered her parents and siblings."

"Did anyone ever prove she was or was not Anastasia?"

"Nothing was proved either way. Some people believed her, but a powerful uncle prevented the rest of the family from accepting her," Kat said. "According to this account, she was genuine." The teen gave a laugh. "Would it not be amazing if my secret was like Anastasia's?" When Kat's American friend didn't answer, she said, "Heather, are you okay?"

"Yes, I'm fine. Sorry about that," she apologized. "Sometimes I just get lost in my thoughts." Actually, Heather didn't think Kat's question was funny or far-fetched. *What if . . . ?* But there were too many *if's* for Heather to share her thoughts. "Anyway, I came in to tell you something about your stolen Bible."

"Has it been found?" she asked eagerly.

"Not yet. Kat, you said there wasn't much in it about your family, didn't you?"

"It only contains the record of my mother's relatives."

"Was there anything at all in there about your father's family?"

"He knew nothing," she snapped. "I have told you that."

"I know," Heather said softly. "I want to make sure I didn't miss anything."

"Please forgive me," Kat apologized. "You are only trying to help. I am full of nerves, though."

"It's okay," Heather soothed. "I would be, too. You see, Kat, the thief might have thought the Bible said something important about your father, and that's why he or she took it. I suspect your father's family had or knew a valuable secret that could be worth a fortune."

"You do?" Her blue eyes sparkled.

"Yes. And we'd better find out what it is. I have a feeling there's a lot at stake."

"I do not know whether to be scared or excited," Kat said.

Neither did Heather.

After dinner the Reeds, Kat, and Jenn drove to Kirby College for the lecture. Heather carried the carefully wrapped cup and saucer in her backpack. They met Brian and Joe at the entrance to the auditorium, and they all sat together.

Heather found the talk fascinating, especially when the professor, Dr. Maria Herzog, spoke of the unrest in Belgravia. There were many questions afterward, but the Reed party left their seats right away so they could get to Dr. Herzog before anyone else. They spotted George Samra in the hallway behind the stage, and after Heather explained her mission, he promised to flag down the lecturer for her.

They waited twenty minutes before gaining access to the middle-aged woman. She was tall and slender and wore her graying hair in a chin-length bob. Heather was intrigued by her resemblance to Kat now that she saw the woman close up.

Joe, never one for subtlety, blurted, "Man, you guys look alike!" Everyone seemed startled by his outburst, and he quickly apologized. "I'm sorry. It's just that Kat looks like you, Dr. Herzog."

The woman smiled tolerantly. "We Europeans tend to look alike in a roomful of Americans."

Heather also noticed that with the professor was a tall, well-groomed man with graying brown hair. *Is it possible he could be the hit-and-run driver?* Heather wondered. *He sure fits the description. But what would he be doing with this professor? She's not the woman who tried to steal Kat's suitcase at the airport.*

"Dr. Herzog, my friend would like to ask you something," George Samra said.

Heather handed the unusual cup and saucer to the professor. "Can you translate the inscription?" she asked.

The professor looked startled when she saw the set. "Where did you get this?"

"At a flea market," Heather said. The woman looked baffled. "That's an outdoor rummage sale."

"This is quite rare," Dr. Herzog said, her gaze darting toward her companion. He was also keenly interested. "The wording on the pieces says they were made in Belgravia."

"What does that 'X' mean?" Joe inquired. "It's just like a symbol on Katarina's ring."

At the mention of the ring, Dr. Herzog searched Kat's eyes. "What ring?"

"It is in a safe-deposit box. I did not feel secure wearing it," the Austrian said.

Kat didn't say why, and Heather was inwardly grateful. *I don't trust these people at all,* she thought.

"How old do you think the cup and saucer are?" Mr. Reed asked.

The professor shook her head. "I cannot say. I would guess they come from this century, though."

"And the 'X'?" Joe persisted.

"It could mean anything," she said quickly, handing the cup and saucer back to Heather.

At that point a college official whisked Dr. Herzog away to a press conference, and she said good-bye. As Brian and Joe walked the others to the car, Brian walked off to the side with his sister.

"I think I've seen that 'X' before," he said quietly. "Look in that book of heraldry I have at home."

"Are you turning sleuth, Brian?" she teased.

"Hardly!" he retorted. "But I care about Katarina. I don't want to embarrass myself if I'm wrong. What I'm thinking is too crazy for words."

"Maybe not," Heather said. "This whole situation is bizarre, right down to Dr. Herzog's resemblance to Kat."

Brian grinned. "Joe's really one for putting his foot in it, isn't he?"

"He sure is," Heather agreed. "But I have to admit, he only said what I was thinking."

"So, what does it all mean?"

"I'm not sure yet."

Mr. and Mrs. Reed insisted on stopping for a snack on the way home. Heather tried to keep up with the conversation, but she was impatient to examine Brian's book. When they finally got home, it was late and everyone else went right to bed. Heather rushed to her brother's room and closed the door.

It took her a few minutes to locate the dog-eared volume Brian had long cherished. She sat on his bed with it and turned on a reading lamp. The inscription inside read, "For Brian Reed, age five, from Dr. and Mrs. Samra." She quickly flipped the pages to the index and, acting on intuition, looked up Belgravia. On the right page, Heather was astonished to see the same "X" that was on Kat's ring and the china set. She read that it stood for the Belgravian royal House of Caroli!

12

A Royal Surprise

Dare I even think it? Was Katarina's father somehow connected to the House of Caroli? Heather asked herself.

She didn't find much information on the Belgravian royal family, so she checked the encyclopedia. Its article on the Carolis proved limited as well.

I know! Heather suddenly thought. *Mr. Michaelson knows Eastern European history really well. I'll ask him about the Carolis in class tomorrow. I can't wait to tell Kat what I've found!*

Although Heather felt terribly excited by her discovery, she was more tired than she realized and quickly fell asleep after turning off her light. Unfortunately the next morning she awakened later than usual. Kat had already left for school, much to Heather's disappointment.

"If you hurry, I'll give you a lift," Mr. Reed offered, quickly drinking his coffee and stuffing papers into his briefcase.

During the brief ride to school, Heather shared her findings. Mr. Reed had turned on the all-news station for traffic reports but kept the volume low enough to hear what Heather was saying.

"I know it may seem far-fetched, but Kat could be royalty!" she concluded.

Her dad's handsome face appeared grave. "Heather, I don't want you building her up only for her to get let down," he cautioned. "You may be on to something, but get some more facts before you tell her anything."

"Okay, Dad," she consented as he pulled up to the school. "I plan to ask my teacher more about the royal family in class today."

"I think that's a good idea."

Just then Heather heard the radio news announcer say something about the Belgravian elections. Quickly she reached for the volume control and turned it up. She and her dad listened carefully as the newsman said Belgravians had voted overwhelmingly to return to a monarchy.

"Imagine what that could mean for Kat!" Heather exclaimed.

"Well, *just imagine it* for now, okay?" her dad advised.

"Okay." When Mr. Reed pulled up to the entrance, Heather kissed his cheek and rushed inside just as the final bell rang.

It seemed an eternity until Global Governments that afternoon. Heather found it especially difficult not to tell Kat what she had discovered. When the period finally arrived, Mr. Michaelson conducted a review for their upcoming test. Heather took the opportunity to ask several questions about the Belgravian royal family. The teacher was only too glad to give her the information she craved.

"The Carolis' history is sad," he began. "Like many Eastern European royal families, the world wars ruined them."

"Who was the last king or queen?" Heather asked.

"Queen," he supplied. "Her name was Sophia, and she died in 1946 when she was only thirty years old. She had just been on the throne for ten years."

"She was young," Heather commented. "How many children did she have?"

"She and her husband, Prince Stefan, had five."

"What happened to them?" a different student asked.

"The German leader Adolf Hitler wanted Sophia to create closer ties with his country. She flatly refused, though."

"Why?" the same student asked.

"Because it would have been Hitler's first step in conquering Belgravia."

She sounds like a courageous woman, Heather thought.

"Eventually a handful of Belgravians who supported Hitler turned the military against Queen Sophia. She and her family fled the country in 1939."

Kat asked, "Where did they go?"

"To Switzerland, which was neutral during World War II."

That's where Kat's father ended up, Heather considered. *I wonder if there's a connection somehow.*

Mr. Michaelson paused then asked impishly, "And what are the dates of that conflict?"

"1939–1945," several students called out together.

"Excellent! Know that for the test. Now then, the queen and her family remained in Switzerland that whole time. Her last son was born there in 1945. When Germany lost the war, Russia crushed Hitler's troops in Belgravia. The queen then returned. The people were overjoyed, but now she had new enemies to defeat."

"Who were they?" Heather asked.

"The Russians. You see, Germany had invaded Russia twice in less than thirty years, and they plowed right through Eastern Europe to do it. After World War II, the Russian leaders said that area should be under their control so Germany wouldn't be able to attack them anymore," Mr. Michaelson explained.

"So the Russians took over Belgravia?" a guy questioned.

"In a manner of speaking. They picked certain Belgravians to rule on Russia's behalf."

"How did the queen die, and what happened to her family?" Heather interrupted.

"That is tragic. She died giving birth to a girl in 1946, and Prince Stefan was outraged. He believed the doctors bungled the delivery on purpose. The queen had always been a healthy, robust woman. Stefan thought he and his children were all in danger."

"What did he do?"

"He tried to smuggle his children out of Belgravia, but only the two youngest made it alive. The oldest one was now the rightful heir to the throne, then his sister. In Belgravia the crown belongs first to the oldest son or daughter, then to his or her oldest son or daughter."

"Prince Stefan must have been heartbroken!" Heather exclaimed.

"Not for long. He was killed shortly afterward in a plane crash. Most historians don't believe it was an accident," he added soberly.

Mr. Michaelson went on with the review, but Heather was thinking about the two royal children who escaped from Belgravia. She wondered what the odds were that Katarina's father might be the missing prince.

Prince Stefan probably changed their names to protect his children. They could have easily blended in with the hundreds of thousands of war orphans at that time. Kat's mysterious ring makes me think her father was the missing prince and that whoever has it is the rightful heir to the throne. Heather inhaled deeply. *Since her father is no longer living, Kat could be Belgravia's new queen!*

She shifted her attention back to Mr. Michaelson, however, when he told the class what had happened in Belgravia just that day.

"The free elections have just been held," he said, "and the people voted to go back to a monarchy. The communists who are still hanging around may not honor the results, however, because there is no available king or queen. You see, what happened to the royal children remains a mystery to this day."

I have a feeling the mystery is about to be solved, Heather thought excitedly.

She only had a few moments to talk to Katarina after class. "I'd like to know something about your father," Heather told her.

"Yes, what is it?"

"How old was he when he died?" she asked gently.

"He was forty-nine." Kat wore a puzzled expression.

Heather did some quick calculating, but before she could share her thoughts, a bell interrupted them.

"Goodness! I must hurry!" the exchange student exclaimed.

"Meet me by the flagpole after school," Heather called after her.

"All right," Kat yelled over her shoulder as she hurried away.

Heather rushed to her last class, excited over this latest piece of information: *Mr. Schiller would have been born in 1945, the same year as the prince!*

By now she was totally distracted. When the last bell finally sounded, Heather quickly pulled the necessary books from her locker and headed for the flagpole where Jenn, Evan, and Pete were talking.

"Have you seen Kat?" she asked.

"Your mom just picked her up," Pete said.

Heather was totally stumped. "She did? I didn't know she was coming for Kat. I wonder why they didn't wait for me."

"Beats me," Jenn shrugged.

"You're sure it was my mom?"

"She was driving the minivan," Evan pointed out.

"Maybe they discussed it this morning. I left later than Kat," Heather mentioned. "Still, it doesn't seem right. Mom would have told me." She suddenly got inspired. "Stay right here! I want to check something, and I may need your help."

They all agreed to wait while Heather raced toward a pay phone inside the school so she could call home. Her mother's secretary, Connie Ball, answered.

"Hello, Doctor Reed's office."

"Connie, this is Heather. Is my mother there?"

"Yes," the woman said, "but she's seeing patients."

"Is the minivan there too?"

"Well, yes."

Before Connie could ask what was going on, Heather thanked her and hung up.

Katarina is in great danger, she thought.

13

Wild Kat Chase

Heather went straight to the school office and asked one of the secretaries if there'd been a message for Katarina Schiller that day.

"I'm not sure," said one.

Then the senior secretary broke in. "Yes, Heather. A message came through from your mom during the last period."

"Would you please tell me what it said, Mrs. Firth?"

"That your mother would be picking Katarina up after school."

"Thank you so much," she said and rushed back to the pay phone. *I don't want them to know what's going on right now,* she determined.

Heather fished in her backpack for a quarter then called the Kirby Police.

"Chief Cullen, someone posing as my mother left a message at school that she would pick Kat up after classes. And Kat fell for it! My friends said a white minivan came for her a few minutes ago."

"This is serious," he said glumly.

Heather quickly told him what she had learned about Belgravian history, ending with the elections. "I think Kat could be next in line to the throne. Apparently these enemies of hers knew it all along and have been trying to get her out of the way."

"That is truly amazing." Cullen became quiet for a few moments then said, "You know, Heather, it's possible that the missing princess, who would be her aunt, is still alive. If so, and she knows who she is, and she knows who Kat is, and she's bent on being queen herself no matter what . . ." his voice trailed off. "It's pretty fantastic, but so is this whole situation."

"So, one of the people threatening Kat could be her aunt," Heather summarized. "Like maybe Professor Herzog. They resemble each other."

"They probably stole another credit card and rented that minivan so Kat would think your mother was driving it. I'll get some people on this right away," the chief said.

"I'd like to check around myself."

"Just take it easy, Heather. I know how you jump into things headfirst."

"I'll be careful," she promised.

Minutes later she rejoined her friends, who were waiting impatiently. Her news startled them.

"This is awful!" Jenn exclaimed.

"We've got to do something," Pete added.

"I wish I had my car today!" Heather moaned.

"Have Bronco, will travel." Evan held out his keys with a smile. "Where do you want to go?"

Her face lit up. "Kirby College. I want to ask Dr. Samra where we can find Professor Herzog."

"Who?" they all chimed in.

"I'll tell you everything on the way there."

The four teens ran to the parking lot and bunched into the Bronco. When they arrived at the history professor's office minutes later, they found him about to leave. Heather breathlessly told him what had happened. "Do you know where Dr. Herzog might be?" she asked.

"Let me think," the professor mused. "She taught a class this morning at 10:45. Then we had a luncheon in her honor. She left at 1:30."

"Where did she go?"

"I think she's supposed to fly home today," Dr. Samra said.

Heather's heart raced. "Do you know where she was staying?"

"Let me check with the secretary." Seconds later he hung up the phone and said, "The King of Prussia Hotel." He offered to call and see if the woman had checked out yet. Dr. Samra quickly learned that she had.

Just then one of the professor's students stopped by. "Oh, excuse me," he said. "I didn't mean to interrupt." He was holding a gray wig.

"That's all right, Sandy," Dr. Samra said. "I'll be ready in a minute." He smiled at Heather and her friends. "The students are going to put on a talent show this weekend, and Sandy will be impersonating me." He paused, looking deeply concerned. "Is there anything I can do?"

"Nothing else right now," Heather said. "Thanks so much."

On the way to the car, she had another brainstorm. The pieces of the mystery were starting to fit together now.

"I've got it!" she cried out. "Evan, let's go to Mrs. Borgoway's."

"That old Russian woman?" he asked.

"Why?" Jenn inquired as Heather started running to the visitor parking area.

"I think she's a phony," Heather stated. She explained what she meant after they jumped into the Bronco and headed for Mrs. Borgoway's apartment. "That student's wig reminded me of the one that, along with a delivery man's costume, was never returned to the shop at the mall."

"Wow!" Pete exclaimed.

"There's more," Heather broke in. "When Jenn, Kat, and I visited Mrs. Borgoway, I noticed a man's trench coat in her hall closet. If she didn't know anyone in the area, as she claimed, why would she have a man's coat around?"

"Heather, are you saying that Mrs. Borgoway is really a guy?" Jenn asked in amazement.

"No, but I think she's connected with that hit-and-run driver from the day we brought Kat home."

"How do you figure?" Evan asked.

"At the airport a woman tried to steal Kat's suitcase. Then a man stole a purse and used his victim's credit card. The card was traced to that driver who banged into us. A man and a woman were in that car."

"So far so good," Pete commented.

"I suspect the same two people were the pizza parlor thieves," Heather added. "The gunman's accomplice probably was the woman from the airport."

"This is unbelievable!" Jenn cried out.

"There's more." Heather was on a roll. "When we had tea at Mrs. Borgoway's apartment and I got up to get the sugar for her, I noticed a box of cookies that had come from a bakery."

"But Mrs. Borgoway said she made them," Jenn cut in.

"She lied," Heather said bluntly. "And since the bomb that was sent to Katarina came in a box of cookies, I think she helped orchestrate that incident."

"How that mind of yours does work!" Pete exclaimed.

Jenn was catching on. "And why was it Mrs. Borgoway who found you unconscious in the mall rest room?" she asked angrily.

"Exactly," Heather stated.

"Are you saying that Mrs. Borgoway is really this woman accomplice and is just pretending to be an old, Russian immigrant?" Evan asked.

"That's what I strongly suspect. Remember, whoever rented the National Delivery uniform also took out a gray wig." Heather was silent for a moment. "You know, last night the guy hanging around with Dr. Herzog fit the description of the man who's been attacking us and Kat."

"Then there's a threesome involved?" Pete asked.

"At least. And I think they've been trying through so-called accidents and thefts to get Kat's ring," she added. "That's what I suspect it takes for a person to prove he or she is the rightful heir to the Belgravian throne."

Minutes later they arrived at Mrs. Borgoway's apartment building, but she wasn't in. Heather located the superintendent's office and asked about the tenant.

"I didn't rent that place to any Mrs. Borgoway," he said. "The Krafts lived there."

I was right! Heather thought. "What do you mean, they *'lived* there'?"

"They moved out about fifteen minutes ago," the burly man said.

"Just the two of them?" she asked.

"Who wants to know?"

"A friend." She tried to sound casual.

"Mr. and Mrs. Kraft, a girl about your age, and another woman," he said.

"Were the Krafts an elderly couple?" Jenn asked innocently.

The man was immediately suspicious. "I thought you were friends," his brown eyes narrowed.

"I am," Heather said quickly. Then she addressed Jenn. "They weren't what I'd call elderly. Maybe in their fifties, wouldn't you say?" she coyly asked the man.

"Yeah, I'd say so."

"Well, I wish they'd have told me they were moving," Heather sighed. Inwardly she felt very excited. "I wanted to say good-bye. Do you know where they were going? We were supposed to see each other again."

"They said something about the airport."

"Thank you. You've been a big help."

"You were right about them, Heather," Jenn said as they got back into the car.

"Obviously they have Kat, and that other woman must be Dr. Herzog," Heather stated.

"What now?" Evan asked.

"Let's go to the bank."

"Huh?" Jenn was perplexed.

"They might still be there," she said. "I have no doubt they're going to get Kat's ring out of the safe-deposit box."

When they got there, however, the foursome learned that Katarina and her kidnappers had just left with the ring. Heather asked to use a phone and called Chief Cullen.

"Nice work, Heather! I'll see to it that the cops at the airport keep an eye out for Kat," he promised.

Pete asked, "What do we do now?"

"One more suspect remains," she announced.

"Who is it?" Jenn queried.

"George Jones," Heather said. "He's often at the scene of a so-called accident, and he's secretive about his identity. Let's go to Martino's."

"My wish is your command!" Evan said.

When they got to the garage, Heather and her friends marched right up to him.

"Where is Katarina?" he asked, looking concerned.

"We were hoping you could tell us," Heather remarked.

"I do not know, but something is wrong, isn't it?"

"She's been kidnapped by three of your associates." Heather's hazel eyes flashed at him accusingly. *I hope this works,* she thought.

"My associates? They are not my . . ." He stopped in the middle of the sentence.

"Then you do know about them!" Heather charged. "How? Tell us quickly. Dr. Herzog and a couple picked up Kat after school. They also have her ring."

"Oh!" he groaned. "It cannot be. Right out from under my nose." He looked like he was in pain.

"What is going on?" Heather demanded.

"I am not one of them," Jones spat. "I was sent here to protect Katarina."

"Sent?" Heather said. "By whom?"

"Important Belgravians who want her family's house restored to the throne. I am *for* her," he stressed. "I have followed the princess like a guardian angel to protect her from her aunt and those maniacs. And just when it looked so good with the outcome of the elections!" He moaned again.

"So, Dr. Herzog *is* her aunt!" Heather said.

"Wait here." Jones wiped his hands and rushed inside to tell his boss he was leaving, and that he would explain it all later. "I know where they might be," he said after returning.

"They're headed for the airport," Pete remarked.

"Yes, and the police are watching for them," Evan added.

"I do not think they have gone there yet. I only pray we are not too late."

14

Happily Ever After

"Let us take my station wagon," Jones directed. "I know exactly where to go."

"Where is that?" Jenn asked.

"A hotel near the Philadelphia city line. Maria Herzog has been staying there for two weeks," he explained.

"But I thought she was only here for her speeches at Kirby College," Heather said.

"And that she was staying in King of Prussia," Pete added.

Jones shook his head as he merged into traffic. "She has been part of the scheme to get rid of the princess from the time Katarina arrived. Maria only stayed at the King of Prussia Hotel for two nights."

"Who is the couple with her?" Heather questioned.

"The Klasinskis. Johann is a medical doctor from Switzerland." Jones grimaced. "He is, as you Americans say, bad news."

"How did all of you get involved in this situation?" Heather asked.

"My name is really George Bolevic," he began. "My family came from Belgravia, but they fled after Queen Sophia was murdered." He paused for a moment and looked both ways in an intersection before continuing their journey, and the conversation. "My grandparents had worked in service to both the queen and her father before his death. They loved the royal family very much."

"Are you royalty?" Jenn's blue eyes widened.

"No," he smiled. "I am a loyal subject, however. I am also a social worker at the orphanage in which Katarina's father and Aunt Maria were raised. Dr. Klasinski also is employed there."

"He is?" Heather was amazed.

"Yes. He is originally from Belgravia, but after graduating from a Swiss medical school, he stayed in that country to work." Jones frowned. "Although he is a brilliant man, Klasinski has an evil streak. Nearly a year ago Maria Herzog came to examine her childhood records. Her husband had died not long before that, and her three children were anxious to know more about their mother's past. They asked her to find out what she could."

"She has three children?" Heather questioned.

"Yes. They are all in Switzerland going to boarding schools," George said. "When I investigated Maria's history, I discovered a handwritten note attached to the last page. It was by a nun who had smuggled the prince and princess into Switzerland. She had known Queen Sophia and her family when they lived there in exile. Mother Anna wrote the story of her noble deed, how she posed as the infants' mother to carry them to safety. The paper was dated two years ago, right before Mother Anna's death."

"Then she never told them their true identity?" Heather assumed.

"That is right. Mother Anna always worried the truth would endanger them. She did not even tell the children they each had a living sibling."

"Is she the one who gave that ring to Mr. Schiller?" asked Evan.

"That is what the message said. He was next in line to the throne, and the ring would be required by Belgravian law to prove his identity if ever he sought the throne," Jones explained.

Jenn was excited. "You were right about that, Heather!"

She nodded. "What did Dr. Herzog do after she found out who she was?"

"First I must tell you that there was more in the note. Prince Stefan had not only used Mother Anna to smuggle his children out of Belgravia. He also took the crown jewels and hid them in a safe place in the palace, one no one but he knew about. Then the prince carefully recorded the exact spot of the pieces and gave the note to Mother Anna." Jones paused. "In reading her last journal entries, I discovered that Mother Anna planned to give Prince Stefan's note to Katarina's father. She had seen the fall of communism in Belgravia and thought the time was right for him to know who he really was. But she died before carrying out her purpose." He sighed.

"It sounds as if this mystery was dormant for years, then just recently came to life," Heather commented.

"Yes, it does to me, too," Jones agreed. "That brings me back to Maria Herzog and Dr. Klasinski. He and I were the people who investigated Maria's records. When we discovered the truth, he swore me to secrecy."

"Why?" Jenn asked.

"He said if the wrong people found out, Belgravia could face even more trouble than it already knew," Jones explained. "Then he and his wife began to plot and scheme with Maria Herzog so she could become the queen. Naturally Klasinski expected a handsome payoff for assisting her, possibly even a powerful position in the new government."

Everyone was intrigued. "Then what?" Heather urged him impatiently.

"Maria went in search of her brother, Josef Schiller. If she could get the ring, she could present herself as the rightful queen if Belgravia ever went back to its former system. If necessary, Klasinski would kill Josef and make his death appear natural. Then Maria found out that Josef had already died and that it was now Katarina who stood between her and the throne."

Heather interrupted him. "Did they ever attack her in Austria?"

He nodded, focusing his gaze on the traffic. "Once. They tried to make her fall from a ladder in a book shop."

"Kat told me about that! How do you know about it?"

"I followed them to Austria, hoping to protect Josef and his heir from Maria's and the doctor's evil ways."

"Why the secrecy?" asked Jenn. "Why didn't you just tell Katarina what was going on in the first place?"

"I am afraid it is not that simple," Jones said. "My friends and I thought it would be best for her not to know her identity until after the elections."

"I'm confused," Evan said. "How did you know about the plot against Kat?"

"One of Maria's children overheard his mother talking to Klasinski about it, and he called the orphanage's mother superior. She asked my advice. I contacted some powerful Belgravian friends who still believe in the House of Caroli. They asked me to guard Katarina from her enemies and, when the time was right, bring her back to Belgravia."

"And if I'm correct, you started following Kat over here when my family and I picked her up at the airport," Heather said.

"You are correct." Jones's shoulders slumped as he said, "I just hope I have not failed the princess."

When they arrived at Maria Herzog's hotel, the parking garage was full. Jones became frustrated as he drove around and around waiting for an available spot. Heather suggested she and the others get out and rush ahead to the professor's room.

"She is in 612," he called after them.

They hurried to the lobby and asked whether Maria Herzog had checked out.

"She's still here," the desk manager said, referring to his computer.

"Thank God!" Jenn exclaimed.

Heather said, "Our friend is in Dr. Herzog's room, and we think she's in danger. Will you please let us in with your pass key?"

The dignified man's eyes narrowed. "Is this some kind of prank?"

"You must believe me," Heather said seriously.

"What if I don't?"

"There's no time to lose. Please call the Kirby Police and ask for Chief Cullen," Heather requested, telling him the number. "He'll verify the story."

"Well, all right," he said after searching her face.

When the manager learned that Heather was telling the truth, he summoned the house detective. Then they all rode the elevator to the sixth floor and hurried down an elegant hallway to the room. Although it was quiet inside, Heather sensed it was not empty. The manager put the key in the lock and turned it. When the door clicked open, the young people gasped. DR. KLASINSKI WAS ABOUT TO STICK A HYPODERMIC NEEDLE IN KAT'S ARM!

"Stop!" Heather yelled at the top of her lungs.

The startled physician was so surprised he dropped the needle. But Maria Herzog calmly aimed a gun at them. Mrs. Klasinski stood off to the side in open-mouthed shock, a gray wig in her hands.

"You will please step inside," Professor Herzog motioned smugly. "And you will drop your weapon," she told the detective, "or I will shoot this young lady." Herzog moved over to Katarina. When they had obeyed, she said mockingly, "This is most unfortunate for you."

"And for you!" a man shouted from the doorway. George Jones stood there, pointing a gun at her. When Dr. Herzog faltered, Heather bravely lunged forward and tripped the woman. Evan pounced in their direction and grabbed the gun while Pete dove after the lethal needle. Jones and the detective tackled Klasinski, preventing his escape.

When Kat's knees buckled weakly from the strain, Jenn helped her to a sofa. To the Austrian's amazement, there next to her, in an open suitcase, lay her stolen Bible.

"It is all over now," Jones announced triumphantly.

Two days later all the Reeds, Jenn, Joe, Evan, and Pete accompanied Katarina to the airport. With her were George Jones (or Bolevic), a State Department official, and a bodyguard.

"I wish we could have had more time together," Kat told her friends, "but I must go back to my country." She paused then added, "It seems strange yet nice to think of Belgravia as my home after growing up in Austria."

"Your father would be so proud of you," Mrs. Reed said warmly. "As we are." She hugged her tightly.

Joe shyly took the princess's hand. "I'll miss you."

"I will miss you too." Kat leaned forward and kissed him on the cheek. "I will never forget you, Joe. Or you, Heather. How can I ever thank you for what you have done?"

"Be the best queen Belgravia ever had," she smiled.

"I may need some advice," Kat teased.

"You know where to find me!" Heather said.

"I want all of you to attend my coronation," the princess announced. Their looks of surprise pleased her. "You will have made it possible, after all."

Heather's eyes were misty as they waved good-bye. "God bless you, Katarina."

"He already has," she replied.